BERNIE & MAGRUDER
THE PIRATE'S TREASURE

Other Aladdin Paperbacks
by Phyllis Reynolds Naylor

BERNIE & MAGRUDER
THE PIRATE'S TREASURE

Phyllis Reynolds Naylor

ALADDIN PAPERBACKS

New York   London   Toronto   Sydney   Singapore

First Aladdin Paperbacks edition October 1999
Revised jacket edition April 2001
Copyright © 1997 By Phyllis Reynolds Naylor
Originally published as *The Treasure of Bessledorf Hill*

Aladdin Paperbacks
An imprint of Simon & Schuster Children's Publishing Division
1230 Avenue of the Americas
New York, NY 10020

Designed by Michael Nelson
The text of this book was set in Goudy.
Printed and bound in the United States of America.

2 4 6 8 10 9 7 5 3

The Library of Congress has cataloged the hardcover edition as follows:
Naylor, Phyllis Reynolds.
The treasure of Bessledorf Hill / Phyllis Reynolds Naylor.—1st ed.
cm.
"A Jean Karl book."
Summary: The people of Middleburg search for buried treasure around Bessledorf Hill and the Bessledorf Hotel.
ISBN 0-689-8337-6 (hc.)
[1. Buried treasure—Fiction. 2. Hotels, motels, etc.—Fiction.
3. Mystery and detective stories.] I. Title.
PZ7.N24Tq 1997
[Fic]-dc20
96-30514
ISBN 0-689-81856-4 (Aladdin pbk)

For Daniel Holtzman

✦

Contents

One
_____

The Bobbing Light

The Bessledorf Hotel was at 600 Bessledorf Street between the bus depot and the funeral parlor. Officer Feeney said that some folks came into town on one side of the hotel and exited on the other. The Bessledorf had thirty rooms, not counting the apartment where Bernie Magruder's family lived, and Feeney said that once, a long, long time ago, a pirate had stayed in one of them.

"Which room was it?" asked Bernie, his eyes wide, as he pedaled along on his bike beside the policeman.

"Now, that I couldn't say."

"How would a pirate get to Indiana?" Bernie continued, still disbelieving. "There aren't any oceans around here."

"Why, Bernie, I'm surprised at you!" the officer said,

tapping at a telephone pole with his nightstick. "The backyard of the Bessledorf Hotel used to reach all the way down to the Middleburg River. The Middleburg River runs into the Wabash, the Wabash flows into the Ohio, the Ohio runs into the Mississippi, the Mississippi empties into the Gulf of Mexico, and the Gulf, as anyone *should* know if he's studied his geography, opens into the Atlantic Ocean. Pirates were everywhere, not just the ocean."

"Wow!" said Bernie.

"Easy enough for a pirate to get to Middleburg, bury his treasure, and sail right out again. So that all those folks along the coast who are looking for buried treasure in caves and coves may just be out of luck."

"Treasure?" cried Bernie, almost riding his bike into a fence in his excitement. "There's *treasure?*"

"Well, now, I didn't say that exactly. Every now and then the story pops up again. Why, I've heard it myself three or four times since I came to Middleburg, but probably it's just talk. A way to pass the time."

Perhaps so, but it was not something Bernie could easily forget. Before the Magruders came to Middleburg, they had blown about the country like dry leaves in the wind, as Mother put it. Now Bernie had grown to like the old hotel, where his father was manager, and hoped they would stay a long time.

"Dad," he said that night as the family ate their dinner in the apartment behind the registration desk. "Do you think it's possible that there could be a treasure right here in this hotel?"

Bernie's father looked around the table where Bernie, Lester, Joseph, Delores, and Mrs. Magruder were sitting and said, "Indeed I do, my boy! The treasure is right here at this table—the most wonderful, magnificent family a man could ever have! A rare collection! Pearls beyond price!"

"I mean *buried* treasure," said Bernie.

"None of us is buried yet that I know of," said twenty-year-old Delores, chewing a celery stick.

"*Pirate's* treasure," said Bernie.

Delores's eyes popped open wide, as did Joseph's and Lester's. "Bernie Magruder, if there's any money buried around here, I want to know about it," his sister said.

"Gold?" squealed Lester, who was nine, and two years younger than Bernie. Lester was eating meat loaf and gravy. Actually, he was eating a big puddle of gravy into which he occasionally dipped a small bite of meat loaf.

"I don't know," said Bernie. "Dad, could we get a piece of gold somewhere and let Mixed Blessing sniff it? Maybe if there was any gold hidden in the hotel, he could lead us to it."

The Great Dane, asleep by the door, gave a happy

little snort at the mention of his name and went on snoozing.

"My dear, dear family," said Theodore. "Let us not gather up for ourselves treasures upon earth where dew and dust doth corrupt and thieves break in and murder us all in our beds."

"Oh, that would make a marvelous plot for my next novel!" said Mother, who wrote romance novels when she wasn't busy at the registration desk or in the hotel dining room. "Beautiful Magnolia Mossgrove could be a woman of unlimited means, but she fears that each new suitor who appears at her door is ultimately after her money."

"Oh, I don't know," said Delores. "If I was a woman of unlimited means, I'd just keep the suitors coming. Wouldn't bother me a bit."

Joseph, the veterinary student in the family, looked across the table at Mother. "What will you call *this* book?" he asked. Already Mother had written a novel called *Quivering Lips* and another, *Trembling Toes*, and mercifully, neither had been published.

Mother thought for a moment. "*The Passionate Pocketbook!*" she said suddenly.

At that exact moment there was a tap on the door of the apartment, and in came Felicity Jones. Felicity was one of the hotel regulars who, along with old Mr. Lamkin and Mrs. Buzzwell, lived in the hotel from month to month and year to year. She was a thin young woman with pale skin and hair, and right now her eyes were as large as coat buttons.

"Mr. Magruder!" she said. "I saw it again! The light—the pale bobbing light—up on Bessledorf Hill!"

Two

Order of Watch

Delores Magruder had a job sewing straps and pounding grommets on parachutes. The parachute factory was right at the end of the street, way up on Bessledorf Hill.

"What you saw, Felicity," she said, "was probably the light at the top of the factory, to keep planes from flying into it in the dark. It's a little red light that blinks on and off from nine in the evening to six the next morning."

"This was not a red light that blinks on and off," Felicity insisted. "This was a pale yellow light that bobbed around farther on down the hill. I've seen it three times in the past week. Now you see it, now you don't."

"There, there, my girl," said Mr. Magruder. "Sometimes we all see or hear things that seem real enough, but . . ."

"Don't 'there, there' me, Mr. Magruder!" said Felicity stiffly. "I know what I see, and what I saw was a pale, bobbing light. If you don't take it seriously, I shall report it to the police myself. Everyone knows the rumor about the pirates' treasure in this town, and it's my hunch the pirates are coming back to claim it."

Bernie knew how his father felt about that. There had already been more happenings at the Bessledorf than Mr. Magruder cared to admit—a mad gasser on the loose (or so they thought); bodies appearing and disappearing in the rooms; a ghost on the stairs; a face in a window of the funeral parlor next door; and bombs in the bus depot. All they needed now was a newspaper story saying that a real loony lived at the Bessledorf Hotel, and Mr. Fairchild, the owner, who lived in Indianapolis, might hear about it, and out the Magruders would go, to blow around the country like dry leaves in the wind.

"Did I say I did not believe you, Felicity?" asked Mr. Magruder, looking shocked. "Did I say that one of my faithful tenants had fabricated a tale in her precious head? No, my dear, I said no such thing. What I am going to do, in fact, is put a member of my family on watch every evening for the next week, and as soon as we see this pale bobbing light that now you see, now you don't, I will personally inform Officer

Feeney, and perhaps then we can give him its exact location."

"Thank you, Mr. Magruder. I trust you are a man of your word."

Theodore Magruder drew himself up to his full height of six foot one. "Indeed I am, my dear, and now, if you will excuse us, we have some meat loaf to attend to."

After Felicity left the apartment, Delores said, "Nice going, Dad. Which of us gets stuck with the loony watch?"

"We shall simply have to take turns, my dear. Each of us will watch for one night and if, at the end of that time, we have not seen the pale bobbing light, I shall simply file it away in my head as another of those UFO sightings, and that shall be the end of it."

"Can we watch television while we're on watch?" asked Lester.

"Why, my boy, if you were an army sentry and even asked such a question, you would be shot," answered his father.

"Well, *I* intend to keep one eye out the window, and the other on my knitting when it's my turn," said Mother.

"I can at least polish my finger- and toenails," said Delores.

"I don't know how I'm supposed to stay up all night and still take my exams," said Joseph. "We are going to be tested next week on the digestive tract of the common house cat, and . . ."

Instantly Lewis and Clark, the two tabbies, set up a howl from the window seat, and Salt Water, the parrot, added a squawk or two.

"We shall go in order of age," their father declared. "I will go first, then Alma, then Delores, Joseph, Bernie, and Lester. All it takes is one sighting to confirm what Felicity has seen, and then the others will not have to stand watch. If that happens, I shall go at once to Officer Feeney, as I said, and we will let the police handle it from there."

"*I* don't mind going on watch!" said Lester. "If I have to sit up all night, I get all the potato chips and pretzels I can eat."

"You will be the last one called, so don't get your hopes up," said his father. "Now, Alma, if you will be so good as to pass the gravy . . ."

The more Bernie thought about it, the more excited he became, and he smiled to himself. When it was his time to go on watch, he would invite his two best friends, Georgene Riley and Weasel, to sit up all night with him. They could each be at a different window of the hotel, and could signal to each other with flashlights if they saw anything—one if by land, two if by sea.

And then he thought of a pirate sailing up Middleburg River—a *modern*-day pirate, in the dead of night—and suddenly he wasn't smiling anymore.

Three

The Parents' Turn

Mr. Magruder sat watch that very night. He had decided that the best place for a lookout was the attic. So he covered the parrot's cage, let Lewis and Clark out into the alley to look for mice, and stepped over Mixed Blessing, who always went to sleep on the mat. Then he locked the door as usual.

After that he said good night to Felicity Jones, Mrs. Buzzwell, and old Mr. Lamkin, who were playing cards in one corner of the lobby. And finally, he took Bernie with him in the elevator to third, where they lowered the folding staircase and went up into the attic.

"Right there, my boy," said Bernie's father, pointing to the window. "You can see out over the whole town from here."

Bernie went to the window and looked. He saw a bus pulling into the station below. He saw Officer Feeney crossing the street at the corner. And on up the street, high on the hill, was the parachute factory where Delores sewed straps and pounded grommets, with its little red light blinking on and off at the very top.

"Well, have a good night, Pop," Bernie told his father. "Wake me if you see anything."

He went back down to the room he shared with Lester in the family's apartment, crawled into the upper bunk, and was shortly asleep, knowing that his father was watching over them from the attic.

He got up once about midnight, however, because he heard one of the cats scratching at the back door, and after he had let Lewis inside, he decided to go to the attic while he was up and see how his dad was doing. He took a flashlight, went up to third, and tip-toed up the folding staircase.

Mr. Magruder was tipped back in his chair, feet on the sill of the little attic window.

"See anything yet?" Bernie asked, shining the light on his father.

Mr. Magruder jumped and blinked. "What?" he asked.

"Have you seen the pale bobbing light?" asked Bernie.

"No indeed, I haven't," said his father. "Haven't

11

taken my eyes off that hill for a moment. Not a trace of a light."

Bernie wasn't so sure. He couldn't sleep anymore, so about three thirty, he got up again. This time, as soon as he reached the top of the folding staircase, he could hear his father's deep snores coming from the chair by the attic window.

Should I wake him? Bernie wondered. And then he asked himself, *Would I wake a sleeping tiger?* So without bothering with the answer, he tiptoed back to bed.

At breakfast the next morning, Mr. Magruder said, "Well, I am happy to report that there was no bobbing light, no pale yellow glow, no haze, no flicker, no illumination at all from Bessledorf Hill, except that which emanates from our glorious globe of a moon."

"Dad," said Lester, "don't you ever speak English?"

"I didn't see a thing," said his father.

Bernie cleared his throat.

"Not a single, solitary glimmer," said Mr. Magruder.

Bernie gave a little cough.

Theodore turned to him. "Do you have something to say, my boy?"

"Only that you don't look very tired for someone who was awake all night," Bernie ventured.

"I feel very well, thank you," said his father. "Tonight your mother will keep watch, and I daresay that if she sees no more than I did, we shall be able, at the end of the week, to assure Felicity that she was mistaken."

"Good luck," said Delores, and went to her job at the parachute factory.

Joseph drove off to the college, and Bernie and Lester walked to school as usual. At recess, Bernie *almost* told Georgene and Weasel what was going on back at the hotel, but decided not to—not yet, anyway—in case word should get out that Felicity Jones was acting a little strange.

"Anything exciting going on at your place?" Georgene asked him as they ate their sandwiches at lunch.

"Only the usual," said Bernie.

"*That* could be anything!" said Weasel.

After school, Bernie and his friends practiced their skateboarding down Bessledorf Street, beginning at the top of the hill near the parachute factory and rolling all the way to the bottom. Bernie looked all around him as he sailed by the factory, but he didn't see anything out of the ordinary—anything that would suggest that someone with a pale bobbing light had been climbing about by the factory.

When Mrs. Magruder took her turn in the attic that evening, Bernie said, "Don't fall asleep, Mom."

"Of course I won't!" she replied. "I am going to spend the night working out the plot of *The Passionate Pocketbook* in my head, and if I see a pale bobbing light on Bessledorf Hill, it will be so much the better."

So Theodore Magruder bade his wife good night,

and Delores went to bed, then Joseph and Bernie and Lester. About four o'clock in the morning, Bernie got up for a drink of water, and went all the way up to third, then up the folding staircase to the attic to see how his mother was doing.

Mrs. Magruder was there by the attic window, just as Bernie's father had been, but she had a clipboard on her lap, a flashlight in one hand, and a pen in the other. The floor was littered with dozens of scribbled pages on which she had been writing a draft of *The Passionate Pocketbook*.

"Ahem!" said Bernie.

Mother jumped, and instantly turned her flashlight off.

"I haven't seen a thing, Bernie," she said. "Not a sign of a light on Bessledorf Hill."

Four

Delores and Joseph Go Next

Delores did not go on night duty without an argument. When Mr. Magruder reminded her at the table that it was her turn to be lookout, she gave a deep sigh.

"I don't know why we should be expected to believe every loony idea that comes along," she told him. "If Felicity Jones thinks she hears voices in the sewer, will we have to crawl down there to find out?"

"Delores, my girl, Felicity may have the brains of a banana, but she also has a mouth like a motor. If we don't take her seriously, the newspapers will. And besides, remember our slogan . . ."

"'The Bessledorf, where beds are best,'" the four children recited aloud.

"And do you know where we would be right now if I didn't have this job as manager?"

"Out in the street!" Delores, Joseph, Bernie, and Lester recited in unison.

"Blowing about the country like dry leaves in the wind," added Mother.

"Right," said Theodore, and placed one hand over his heart. "The Bessledorf Then, the Bessledorf Now, the Bessledorf Forever."

"So help me God," said Delores.

"And *you*, my girl," added her father, "will go on watch tonight *proud* to be the daughter of the man who runs the Bessledorf; *proud* to be the daughter of the woman who is married to the man who runs the Bessledorf; *proud* to be—"

"The sister of the brother of—" said Bernie.

"I'll *do* it! I'll *do* it!" shrieked Delores. "Now let me alone."

So when the clock struck eleven, Delores went to the folding staircase that led to the attic, and the rest of the family went to bed.

Bernie did not sleep well, however. He worried that perhaps there really *was* a pale bobbing light on Bessledorf Hill and none of the family would see it. His tossing around woke Lester, who was in the bunk beneath him.

"Bernie," came Lester's voice.

"Yeah?"

"Are there any more pirates in the world?"

"I don't know," Bernie told him. "I don't think so."

"If a pirate ever came to Middleburg and took me away and asked for ransom, would you pay it?"

"Sure," said Bernie. "If it wasn't over ten dollars. But don't worry. Pirates only take stuff that's important."

"Oh," said Lester.

About one in the morning, Bernie knew he would not sleep at all unless he went to the attic to check on his sister. He crept quietly out of bed, through the apartment, up the stairs to third, and then up the folding staircase to the attic. Delores was sitting in the chair by the window, her feet on the sill, polishing her toenails and listening to her Walkman.

"Delores!" said Bernie sternly, walking over to where she could see him.

Delores jumped, then took off her earphones. "Listen here, Bernie!" she said. "I've been staring out that window half the night, and there's not a thing bobbing around on Bessledorf Hill except Felicity Jones's imagination. Why her mother turned that poor girl loose on the world is more than I can see."

"But what if there *was* a light, and you missed it?"

"What if there was?" said Delores. "Am I supposed to yell and scream? Does Dad think that all the Magruders will go charging up the hill in the dead of night, just because some poor soul who can't sleep is probably taking a little walk with a flashlight?"

Bernie wasn't sure *what* they were supposed to do if

they saw something, but he was disappointed in his sister. And when she announced at breakfast that she had seen nothing, nothing at all, Bernie followed his older brother into the bathroom to brush his teeth.

"Joseph," he said. "Dad went to sleep, Mom wrote her book, Delores painted her toenails, and none of them saw a thing. You'll keep a good watch, won't you?"

Joseph turned to Bernie, his mouth full of toothpaste. "Why are you so interested in that light, Bernie?" he asked.

Bernie sloshed water around in his mouth three times and then spit. "Because . . . because it might be a signal," he said.

"A signal for what?"

"For pirates."

"Bernie! I'll bet Feeney's been putting ideas in your head again. You'll believe anything he says."

"Not everything, Joseph. But what if he *was* right?"

Joseph laughed. "Don't worry. I'm a night owl. When I'm on emergency duty at the veterinary college, I can go thirty hours sometimes without sleep. If there's a light bobbing around on Bessledorf Hill, I'll see it."

That evening, however, Joseph did not come home to dinner. He was not home in time to watch his favorite program on television, and at eleven o'clock, Mother was just about to call the veterinary college

18

when Joseph dragged in with the news that he had helped with a six-hour operation and was so tired he could hardly stand. He took his watch in the attic, but when Bernie checked on him, he was sprawled out on his back, sleeping like a dead man.

Bernie knew right then that if anyone was going to see a light on Bessledorf Hill, it would have to be Georgene, Weasel, and himself.

Five

Making Plans

At long last it was Bernie's turn. *He* would not fall asleep, write a book, or paint his toenails when he was supposed to be on watch. If there was any light on Bessledorf Hill, he would see it. If there was any bobbing about, he'd be the first to notice.

He was just leaving for school that morning when Felicity Jones stopped him in the lobby.

"Bernie," she said, "is anything being done about the bobbing light on Bessledorf Hill? I saw it again last night, and if your father doesn't take it seriously, Officer Feeney will."

"We take it very seriously, Felicity," Bernie told her. "It's possible that for just a moment, when Joseph was on watch last night, he was distracted and didn't see the light, but I promise you that the person on watch tonight won't turn his head for a moment; won't even blink."

Lester was still at the table having a second doughnut, so Bernie left without him. And when he reached the school building, Georgene Riley and Weasel, Bernie's two best friends, were waiting for him on the school steps as they did every morning. As they all went inside, Bernie whispered, "O.T.," which was their code to meet under the oak tree at recess for something important.

When the bell rang after social studies class, Bernie, Georgene, and Weasel sprang from the classroom like chickens from a coop and raced to the big oak tree in one corner of the playground.

"What is it?" Georgene asked, her eyes shining with adventure, her ponytail sticking out high off her neck like a long ear on the back of her head.

"What's the secret?" asked Weasel, his glasses slipping down off his nose as usual.

"You're spending the night at my house," Bernie began, "only nobody is going to sleep, unless we do it in shifts." And then he told them about Felicity seeing a bobbing light on Bessledorf Hill, and how they had to be sentries on watch.

He had thought they would be excited. He had thought they would jump at the chance to sit at the window in his attic in the dark.

Georgene wrinkled up her nose. "Why would I

want to do *that*, Bernie? Why would I want to stay up all night just sitting in your attic?"

"Yeah, watching out the window for a light!" said Weasel. "What's the big deal about that?"

Bernie stopped and thought about it. What *was* the reason he was so excited? Then he remembered what Officer Feeney had said about pirates.

"Because I think it might be pirates," he said in a whisper.

Georgene was still looking at him as though he had just grown spinach for hair.

"Officer Feeney said that once, a long time ago, a pirate stayed at the Bessledorf Hotel," Bernie told them.

Now Weasel was looking at Bernie as though he had spinach for hair. "How would a *pirate* get to Middleburg, Indiana?"

"Why, Weasel, I'm surprised at you!" Bernie said. "He'd sail right up Middleburg River. The Middleburg runs into the Wabash, the Wabash runs into the Ohio, the Ohio runs into the Mississippi, the Mississippi runs into the Gulf of Mexico, and there, as *anyone* should know if he's studied his geography, the Gulf empties into the Atlantic Ocean, and there were pirates all over the place."

"Wow!" said Weasel, his eyes wide.

"Easy enough for a pirate to get to Middleburg, bury his treasure, and sail right out again."

But Georgene was not impressed at all. "Bernie, you are absolutely nuts! You think a modern-day pirate has sailed into Middleburg and is over there on Bessledorf Hill trying to bury his treasure?"

"No, I think somebody might have found a map of where a pirate *once* buried something and is over there at night trying to find it without anyone seeing him," Bernie told her.

"Now *that's* more like it!" said Georgene. "Sure, Bernie, we'll come. I'll tell Mom we're working on a project."

"A *deluxe* project," said Weasel. "I'll tell mine that Bernie Magruder needs a little help."

"And I'll tell mine that you guys are coming for a sleep-over, and maybe she'll get Mrs. Verona to make us some brownies," Bernie said.

"With chocolate chips," added Georgene.

"And chocolate ice cream," said Weasel.

The nice thing about staying overnight with a friend whose father manages a hotel, Bernie's friends always said, was that the cook made you something a little special.

"Mother," Bernie said that evening. "Since I'm on watch tonight, Georgene and Weasel are coming over to sit up with me, just in case I fall asleep. Could Mrs. Verona bake us some brownies?"

"A good idea," his mother said. "If no one sees the light tonight, then I think we can simply tell Felicity

23

to drink a little warm milk before she goes to bed and see if that doesn't take care of the problem."

"And if we *do* see a light?" said Bernie.

"Then tell your father about it, of course," said Mother.

But Bernie wasn't sure what he would do. If he and his friends saw a bobbing light, would he really tell his father, or would they very quietly get a flashlight, creep outside, and make their way to Bessledorf Hill?

Six

Into the Attic

When Bernie got home from school, Mrs. Verona, the cook, was making cookies. Bernie went into the hotel kitchen and peered into the big bowl where she was mixing the dough.

"What kind of cookies are they?" he asked.

"Sugar cookies," she said, and went on beating the dough with her wooden spoon. Mrs. Verona had long, dark hair, which she wore piled on top of her head, fastened with a red comb. She had a little black mole on one cheek, which she called her beauty mark, and very red lips in the shape of a heart.

"Do you think you'll be making any brownies today?" Bernie asked.

"No, today it will be sugar cookies," she said.

"Do you think," asked Bernie, "that you could—

well—put some chocolate chips in the dough?"

"Well, I don't see why not," she said, and dipped one hand in a sack of chocolate chips, sprinkling them heavily throughout the creamy white dough.

"What would happen if you added a little cocoa to the dough?" Bernie asked.

"*Chocolate* chocolate-chip sugar cookies?" Mrs. Verona said, puzzled. "Well, I suppose that can be done." And she scooped up some cocoa and mixed it in.

"Do you think," asked Bernie, "that you could set aside a dozen for Georgene, Weasel, and me?"

"Why not?" said the cook, and ten minutes later, a large pan of round, flat, chocolate chocolate-chip sugar cookies was going into one of the big ovens in the hotel kitchen.

"Well, my boy," said Theodore at dinner, "will you go on watch tonight so that we may get this ridiculous business behind us? If we can tell Felicity Jones that we have spent every hour of every night this past week watching for her bobbing light, then perhaps she will forget about it."

"And perhaps she won't," said Delores. "Next thing you know she'll be seeing green lights or blue lights or hearing bells or something. I tell you, Dad, she was probably dropped on her head as a baby, and the reason her parents pay for her to live here at the Bessledorf is to keep her as far away from them as possible."

"Delores, my girl, be generous for once," said her father. "There was many a time when you were a baby that I was tempted to drop you on your head, but didn't." He looked at Bernie again. "Well, son?"

"I'm ready," Bernie told him. "Georgene and Weasel are coming over too, and we're going to watch in shifts."

"All the better," said Theodore.

"If they don't see the bobbing light, will it be my turn next?" asked Lester, the youngest Magruder of all.

Mr. and Mrs. Magruder exchanged looks. "Let's hope that by then something definitive has turned up that, in the pale light of day, looks less malicious and more benign than it did under cover of darkness," said Theodore.

Lester looked at Bernie. "What did he say?"

"He said we'd probably find out tonight whatever it is."

At nine o'clock, Weasel arrived with his sleeping bag, and not long after that, Georgene.

They played Chinese checkers on the floor of the lobby beside Mixed Blessing, who snorted occasionally and scratched for fleas.

They waited until old Mr. Lamkin had finished watching *Famous Shipwrecks* on television, and Felicity and Mrs. Buzzwell had ended their card game at a table in the corner and gone to bed. One by one the last guests left the hotel restaurant across the lobby, the waiters swept the floor, and Mrs. Verona went home. Then it was time to put the cover on the parrot's cage.

Weasel and Georgene always liked that job, because Salt Water usually said good night to them.

"Good night, beautiful," Georgene said to the red, green, and yellow parrot.

"Good night, beautiful," squawked the parrot in reply.

"Good night, beautiful," said Weasel, mimicking Georgene.

"Good night, mudface," said Salt Water.

Lewis scratched on the front door and, as soon as Bernie let him in, walked through to the back and meowed to be let out again. Then Clark scratched at the back door and, as soon as Bernie let him in, walked through the lobby and meowed to get out the front.

At last Joseph put down his books and went to bed. Delores came home from a date with the butcher's son, Mother turned out the light behind the registration desk, and Father locked the front door.

Bernie, Georgene, and Weasel took their sleeping bags into the hotel elevator, rode it to third, and then climbed the folding staircase into the attic of the hotel. They put a chair in front of the window facing Bessledorf Hill and sleeping bags on either side of it.

"Who wants to watch first?" asked Bernie.

"I will," said Weasel.

Georgene settled down in her sleeping bag and Bernie crawled into his. He didn't think he could sleep at all, however, because Weasel was eating a bag of pretzels, which made a lot of noise.

Suddenly, though, he opened his eyes and realized he had been asleep after all, for Weasel and Georgene were trading places. Weasel gave Georgene the chair he had been sitting in, and now she would watch from midnight till three, and then Bernie from three to six.

"Did you see anything?" he heard Georgene whisper to Weasel.

"Nothing," Weasel replied.

Bernie closed his eyes again and dreamed that the moon was over the water on the Middleburg River, and coming upriver in the moonlight was a ship with a skull-and-crossbones flag on the mast.

Seven

Sure Enough

At three o'clock, Bernie took his place as night watch at the attic window. Georgene was soon fast asleep in her sleeping bag on one side of him, Weasel asleep on the other side.

It was as dark as chocolate pudding outside the window. Now and then Bernie could see a glint of moon as it ducked in and out of the clouds, but mostly, Bernie decided, being on watch was simply boring. Very, very boring.

They had already divided up the cookies Mrs. Verona had made for them. In fact, Bernie had eaten his four in the first fifteen minutes they had been in the attic. Maybe, he thought, if he simply willed it, a bobbing light would appear. If he just put his mind to it and *thought*, maybe he could make it happen.

Shine, he thought to himself. *Please shine*.

But a half hour went by, then fifteen minutes more. From somewhere beyond the window he heard the clock on the town hall strike four.

"Shine," he whispered, his eyes never leaving the window. "Shine, shine, shine." Another hour went by.

Maybe Felicity was nuts. Maybe she'd seen a firefly or car lights or something—a flash of lightning, perhaps. And then . . . just when Bernie was sure he would never trust anything again that Felicity told him, he saw a faint light, a yellow light, a bobbing light—a faint, yellow, bobbing light on Bessledorf Hill.

Bernie's eyes popped open wide and he sat up straighter. Sure enough. The light blinked and bobbed again. A blinking, bobbing light. He leaned forward. Up and down, back and forth the light went, as though carried by someone going up or down the slope of Bessledorf Hill.

With his right foot, Bernie nudged Georgene. With his left, he nudged Weasel.

"Get up," he whispered. "Come here and look."

"What time is it?" asked Weasel.

"Almost five."

Sleepily Georgene and Weasel sat up, and slowly they crawled over to the window.

"It's there!" Georgene said. "There *is* a light!"

Weasel gave his head a shake to force himself awake.

31

"Felicity wasn't kidding, Bernie, there's a light! Now what do we do?" Weasel said.

"Go see what it is," said Bernie. "Bring your jackets and come on."

Leaving their sleeping bags behind, they crept down the folding staircase to the third floor, took the elevator to the lobby, and then, stepping over Mixed Blessing, who was asleep on the mat, they unlocked the front door, stepped outside, and went softly up the sidewalk.

"We forgot a flashlight!" Georgene said after they'd gone a block.

"If we go back, someone might hear," Bernie said, disgusted with himself. "Let's just keep going and see what's up there. Maybe it's better that we don't have a flashlight; we don't want anyone to know we're coming."

All three of them kept their eyes on Bessledorf Hill as they went, and Bernie was disappointed because they did not see the light bobbing again. He hoped they hadn't just imagined it—that they had wanted so badly to see a light that the light they saw was all in their heads.

The problem was that Bessledorf Hill was big. It wasn't just a little hump at one end of town; it was a *big* hump, with houses halfway up it, the parachute factory beyond that, and the rest was public park all the way to the top. The light could have been anywhere.

The only thing Bernie knew for sure was that the light would be on the side facing the hotel, or he wouldn't have seen it at all.

"Whoever it was, he's not there now," said Weasel when they'd walked as far as the parachute factory.

"I think it was over this way," said Bernie, leading them to the side of the hill in the park where the grass had worn away. In winter, the children of Middleburg took their sleds here to Bessledorf Hill and rode to the bottom. But in summer, they often arrived with large sheets of cardboard and would slide down the steep grassy side of the hill. And each time someone slid down the grass, it got slicker and slipperier, until it was almost a slide in itself. By the end of summer, though, there was often no grass left at all.

"If you see anything unusual, let me know," Bernie told his friends, feeling his way along and sliding each foot out ahead of him to tell where he was going.

"We can hardly see *anything*, Bernie! It's too dark," said Weasel.

Bernie started up the steep slope. "It's getting lighter all the time. Keep looking."

They did. They tried staring through the darkness until Bernie felt his eyes would pop out of his head, but he could make out nothing unusual.

"Maybe if we come back in daylight, we'll find footprints," Bernie said to Georgene, who was walking beside him. Turning in Weasel's direction, he started to ask a question, then sensed that his friend wasn't there.

"Weasel?" he said. And then, more loudly, "*Weasel?*"

"Down here," came a voice, and Bernie stared down into the darkness to see a dark shape on the ground. The shape was Weasel.

"What's wrong?" Bernie asked, kneeling down.

"I stepped in a hole!" Weasel said. "One minute my left foot was up beside yours and the next it was down in this hole."

Bernie got down on his hands and knees and felt around. "It's a hole, all right," he said to Georgene. "Someone's been digging here. There's a big pile of dirt . . ."

And then he stopped, for *Georgene* was missing.

"Georgene?" he called softly.

"Over here," she said. "Another hole, Bernie!"

"*Somebody's* been digging around up here," Bernie declared.

"Even a rabbit could have figured that out," Georgene told him.

"Maybe it *was* a rabbit!" said Weasel. "A giant rabbit!"

"Right. A giant rabbit carrying a shovel and lantern," said Bernie. "All I mean is that—" But he didn't finish, because the next thing he knew, *he* had stumbled and fallen into a hole.

Eight

Peg Leg

It was about three feet deep and two feet wide, and, in the early dawn, Bernie could make out Georgene and Weasel, each sticking up out of *their* holes. They all looked like gophers. They *felt* like gophers.

"Are we supposed to squeal or something?" Georgene said dryly.

"Who do you suppose *made* all these holes?" said Weasel, awkwardly crawling out. He sat on the ground rubbing his ankle.

"This is right where the light would have been," said Bernie. "Whoever was walking around with a bobbing light was digging these holes, I'm sure of it."

"But why?" asked Weasel.

"Buried treasure, what else!" said Georgene.

The sky was beginning to lighten. Down in the

business district, the buildings were just becoming distinct through the fog.

"If we got down on our hands and knees and searched the ground, we might find a clue," said Bernie. "A tobacco can, a shoe, a flashlight, a gun . . ."

"Sure, Bernie, sure," Georgene told him. "Maybe we'd even find a shovel with a little tag on it that said, 'This belongs to Peg Leg, who buried treasure here two hundred years ago.'"

"Do you have a better idea?" Bernie asked.

"No . . ."

"Then start searching," said Bernie.

All three of them got down on their hands and knees and began feeling around the bare ground with their fingers. Bernie knew that if Mother was up when he got back to the hotel, he'd have to explain why his pants were so dirty, but he didn't care.

He couldn't feel anything unusual on the ground, however. No pieces of gold, no tobacco cans, not even a flashlight battery.

And then his fingers disappeared. Bernie stopped. His fingers were in a hole. He could feel it. A small hole. A round hole, about two inches wide and three inches deep.

He felt around some more.

"Hey!" came Weasel's voice. "Over here! I found another hole. It's about—"

"Two inches wide and three inches deep," finished Georgene. "I found one too."

"They're all over the place!" said Bernie, searching farther.

"Just exactly the right size for a peg leg—from a pirate," Georgene told him.

"A pirate digging holes in the dirt," said Weasel.

"Hey guys, I'm not kidding this time," said Georgene. "It really *is* just the right size hole for a man with a wooden leg."

They were quiet a moment.

"What do you think we should do?" said Weasel.

"I don't know. Come back again, I guess, and see what . . ."

Suddenly Bernie felt a big hand on the back of his shirt, and at the same time he heard a yelp from Georgene, and then he and Georgene and Weasel were bumping heads as they were lifted to their feet.

"Now what the ding dong are *you* kids up to so early in the morning?" came Officer Feeney's voice. "I *thought* I heard voices when I made my rounds by the parachute factory!"

Bernie, whose legs had turned to rubber momentarily, tried to think of a good excuse. "Looking for bugs," he said.

"Digging for worms," said Georgene.

"Bird watching," said Weasel.

Officer Feeney let go, but continued to stare at them through the morning fog.

"What the blazes are you doing up here? *Look* at

these holes, would you? I know three young folks who are about to catch a whupping from their dads."

"We didn't *do* it!" Bernie said. "We only came up here because we saw a light . . ." And then he knew he was going to have to tell Officer Feeney the whole story, so he did.

He expected the policeman to laugh. Expected him to frown. Expected Officer Feeney to say he had never heard anything so ridiculous in his life.

Instead, Feeney crouched down on the ground, his chin in one hand. "Peg Leg," he said, as if to himself.

Bernie and his friends stared.

"There really *is* a pirate?" Bernie asked.

"It's how the story goes," said Feeney. "We weren't going to say anything, but the police department's been finding these notes around, see. Pieces of paper stuck in odd places, all of them signed by P.L."

"How do you know it stands for Peg Leg?" asked Georgene.

"And how do you know he's a pirate?" asked Weasel.

"Well, I don't know anything for sure. What we *do* know, 'cause we've done some checking, is that the pirate who was *said* to have sailed up Middleburg River, and was *said* to have stayed at the Bessledorf Hotel, was George Tupper, a high-seas bandit, better known as Peg Leg, because he'd lost half a leg at sea."

"How?" asked Georgene, her eyes wide.

"How do I know? I wasn't there!" said Feeney. "Maybe a shark chewed it off. But the notes keep talking about Bessledorf Hill, the northeast corner, and I've more or less had my eye on it. Didn't see anyone coming or going that looked the least bit suspicious to me. But now that you've seen a light, and now that I've seen these holes, well, it's the last thing I want to see in the newspaper, I'll tell you that."

"Why?" asked Bernie.

"Because every man, woman, and child in Middleburg that isn't lame or blind and can carry a shovel will be up here on this blinkin' hill looking for what Peg Leg himself can't find, that's why."

"But even if there *was* a pirate, he wouldn't still be alive," said Bernie.

"You can never tell about pirates," said Feeney. "You can never tell who's got a peg leg. And of course, his great-great-great-great-great-great-grandkids might know where that treasure's buried. What I want from you, now, is a promise that you won't tell *any*one what you've found up here, till I can check this out myself."

The children promised, but it did no good, because when the paper was delivered to the Bessledorf Hotel the following day, the headlines read, PIRATE RETURNS TO MIDDLEBURG.

39

Nine

Landlubber's Delight

"What is the meaning of this?" Bernie's father said at breakfast when he saw the headlines. "How did the story of the bobbing light get in the newspaper? And what's all this about pirates?"

But before anyone could answer, Mrs. Buzzwell appeared at the door to the Magruder apartment.

"Everyone's talking about it, Mr. Magruder," she said.

"Evidently," said Bernie's father.

"I heard it from Felicity Jones myself. She said that if no one else would take her seriously, the newspapers would."

"Oh, no!" cried Mother.

"I don't know why you thought you should keep all this secret," Mrs. Buzzwell buzzed on. "If Felicity has seen a bobbing light on Bessledorf Hill, then I think we should all know about it."

"My dear Mrs. Buzzwell, why do you think that a bobbing yellow light on Bessledorf Hill should be anyone's business other than the one who is doing the bobbing?" asked Theodore, trying to keep his temper.

"Pirates, Mr. Magruder!" the woman cried. "They could come up the Middleburg River and murder us in our beds right here in the Bessledorf Hotel, and we'd never even know it. Or they could march us down to the river and make us walk the plank."

"And how, my dear, do you plan to protect yourself against them, now that you know, or think you know, that pirates are swarming into town?" Theodore asked her.

Mrs. Buzzwell reached into her purse and held up a decal. Bernie stared. It was a picture of a pirate's head, with its three-cornered hat, and a skull and crossbones on the front. A diagonal red line ran through it.

"I'll put this on my door," said Mrs. Buzzwell. "No pirates allowed. I bought two, and the other will go on my window."

"Oh, boy! That'll scare 'em away all right!" said Lester.

"Is everyone in this town crazy, or do they just seem that way?" asked Delores. "Is this a hotel for nut cakes?"

"Laugh if you must," said Mrs. Buzzwell, "but if

someone digs up the treasure, you won't laugh then, I'll wager."

"Treasure?" cried Delores. "Treasure, as in M-O-N-E-Y?"

"Precisely. Everyone wants to know where the treasure's buried, and I have heard that people are arriving in Middleburg by the busload."

At that precise moment the phone rang, and Theodore answered.

"Yes, Mr. Fairchild," he said, and Bernie's heart sank. It was important to keep the owner of the hotel happy. If Mr. Fairchild did not think Mr. Magruder was doing a good job as manager, the family might be out on the street again, blowing about the country like dry leaves in the wind. If he found out that it was Felicity Jones, one of the hotel regulars, who was helping to spread the rumor about a pirate, well . . . Bernie didn't know what Mr. Fairchild might do.

He didn't have to guess what the owner was saying, however, because the man talked so loud that Mr. Magruder had to hold the receiver away from his ear. Bernie could hear every word:

"Theodore, what's this I hear about pirates in Middleburg, and some pale yellow light?" Mr. Fairchild boomed.

"I'm afraid the rumors have gotten out of hand, sir, and there's not much we can do," said Bernie's father.

"Not much you can *do!*" Mr. Fairchild roared. "Not

much you can *do*? My good man, I know that gold seekers are arriving by the busload. They need a place to sleep. They need a place to eat. I want an ad in the newspaper. I want a banner on the canopy over the door. I want every treasure-seeking, pirate-peeking, money-reeking tourist who steps off the bus at the bus depot to know that he is welcome in my hotel."

"Y-yes, sir," said Theodore, as the family stared.

"I want swizzle sticks shaped like peg legs. I want pirates' kerchiefs sold in the hotel lobby. What are you having for dinner in the hotel restaurant tonight?"

"For dinner, sir?" said Bernie's father.

"Tell him salmon with dill, veal with mushrooms, and chicken pot pie," Mother whispered.

Theodore repeated it to Mr. Fairchild.

"No, no, no!" the owner said. "You are *not* having salmon, veal, and chicken, you are having Pirate Specials! You are having Davy Jones's Favorite, Land-lubber's Delight, and Buried Treasure! Change the menus. Order the swizzle sticks! Set up a booth by the registration desk to sell eye patches and kerchiefs and three-cornered hats. And keep those rumors circulating, understand?"

"Perfectly," said Mr. Magruder, and slowly hung up the phone.

"This hotel is *owned* by a nut cake!" Delores declared.

It was all anyone talked about at school on Monday.

The newspaper said that after the bobbing light had been reported on Bessledorf Hill by a young woman living at the hotel, a reporter had investigated and found numerous holes dug all over the northeast slope, and smaller holes just the right size for a peg leg.

When Bernie got home that afternoon, there was a large banner attached to the hotel canopy over the front door.

TREASURE HUNTERS WELCOME, it said.

Taped to the glass on the front door was the evening menu: *Davy Jones's Favorite, Landlubber's Delight, and Buried Treasure, à la carte*.

Inside the lobby was a booth next to the registration desk, selling all kinds of pirate souvenirs. And there on the rug was Mixed Blessing, the Great Dane, with an eye patch over one eye. On the sofa were the two cats, Lewis and Clark, wearing kerchiefs about their necks. And pacing back and forth on his perch was Salt Water, the parrot, wearing a black three-cornered hat with a skull and crossbones on the front.

Ten

Pirate Craze

The town of Middleburg was going wild. Every day the buses coming into the depot next door to the hotel carried more and more people, and every single room at the Bessledorf Hotel was filled, something that had not happened since a ghost had been seen in one of the rooms.

Every store in town put a picture of a pirate in its advertisements. Every store sold something that a pirate might wear. It even looked as though knee breeches and buckles might come back into style. The hardware store on the corner had a huge chest in the window, filled to overflowing with fake gold coins.

GUESS THE NUMBER OF COINS AND WIN AN ELECTRIC DRILL, read the sign above it.

The sidewalks were so crowded that sometimes

Bernie had to walk on the grass to get around the people who walked three and four abreast. And of course skateboarding was out of the question completely.

"What this town needs is a real pirate ship sailing up the Middleburg River and blasting it to smithereens with a cannon!" Delores complained at dinner.

"Well, you, my dear, would be the first to go, with the parachute factory sitting there near the top of the hill like a sitting duck," her father told her.

"People are everywhere!" Delores continued. "They tap on the windows of the factory. They open the door and walk right in. Somebody started the rumor that what we really make are sails for pirate ships, and now the owner has started giving tours. Why, I sewed all my straps on backward today, and pounded the grommets on upside down."

"Pity the poor chap who has to use that parachute," said her father. "Remember that your work is the window to your soul."

"Ha! If I could choose my own life, I wouldn't be doing any work at all!" Delores declared. "I would be lying on a beach in a diamond-studded dress, and a handsome man with a black mustache would be kissing my hand."

"Then anyone looking for your soul would find emptiness." Theodore sighed. "Build not your house upon the sand, my girl, for it can only lead to a bridge over troubled water."

When Bernie got to school the next day, he found that the pirate craze had even invaded the classroom. The list of spelling words for the week was: *treasure*, *galleon*, *stowaway*, *privateer*, *Barbary*, *ruffian*, *buccaneer*, and *plunder*.

In English, the teacher began reading *Treasure Island* to the class. In math, they studied old coins and "pieces of eight." And in history, the class divided into groups, and each group had to give a report on either Captain Kidd, Blackbeard, or Jean Laffite.

When Bernie arrived home that afternoon, Georgene and Weasel with him, they could scarcely get into the lobby, for people were offering to pay fifteen dollars just to put their sleeping bags on the floor, so eager were they to go treasure hunting.

The police chief and the mayor, however, had other ideas. They had posted signs all over Bessledorf Hill saying NO DIGGING ALLOWED. But it did no good. Next they built a fence around the park on Bessledorf Hill. People simply climbed over the fence.

Finally, the police chief and mayor put their heads together and realized that if they started fining people for digging, the treasure seekers would all leave Middleburg, and business would suffer.

So the next morning, the newspaper said that digging would be allowed on the north slope of Bessledorf Hill on Mondays and Thursdays, on the east slope on Tuesdays and Fridays, on the south slope on Wednesdays and Saturdays, and Sundays were reserved for the west.

What Bernie and his friends discovered, however, was that after the digging hours were over for the day, along about dark, the city maintenance crews would move in and fill the holes back up again, so that when one wave of treasure hunters gave up and left town, there would be new places for the rest to dig.

"But how do they know the treasure is buried right here on this hill?" Georgene asked, as she and Bernie and Weasel were adjusting the neckerchiefs on Lewis and Clark. Weasel had taught Salt Water to say, "Ahoy, mates!" and now nobody could shut him up.

"One evening when Officer Feeney was walking his beat, he noticed that there was a piece of rolled-up paper stuck in the fence railing around the funeral parlor each day," Bernie told her. "Since it looked like a private note to someone, he didn't touch it, and every morning, when he started his rounds again, the paper would be gone. But one day he got curious and read one of the notes. It said, 'So. slope, no luck. Try N 10, W 2, 6 under. P.L.'"

"How would anyone know what that's supposed to mean?" asked Weasel.

"Well, Feeney says it's pretty straight pirate talk. He says it means, 'South slope no luck. Try going ten paces north, then two west, and dig down six feet. Peg Leg.'"

"What did Feeney do once he read the note?" asked Georgene.

"Put the note back, and the next day when he checked out Bessledorf Hill, there was the hole six feet under, in the exact location the note had said."

"Then maybe the treasure has already been found and taken away!" Georgene suggested.

"He doesn't think so, because more notes keep coming, only they're in different places now. In fact, Feeney's been taken off his usual beat, and his new job is just to watch for messages."

At that moment there was the sound of footsteps on the back porch leading into the hotel apartment where Bernie and his friends were eating cheese crackers, and a moment later a deep voice said:

> *"Fifteen men on the dead man's chest—*
> *Yo-ho-ho, and a bottle of rum!*
> *Drink and the devil had done for the rest—*
> *Yo-ho-ho, and a bottle of rum!"*

Eleven

The Stranger

The next thing Bernie knew, a man in a pirate's hat, with a red sash around his waist and a patch over one eye, was knocking at the back door of the hotel apartment. Bernie could see him through the glass.

He swallowed, then got up and went to answer.

"Yo-ho-ho!" said the man again. And then he laughed and took off his eye patch.

"Mr. Fairchild!" Bernie squeaked.

"Just having a little fun, Bernie. Decided if there were pirates sailing into Middleburg, I might as well be part of the action. How's business?"

"Really good," Bernie told him. "All our rooms are filled."

"Excellent! Excellent!" said Mr. Fairchild, rubbing his hands with pleasure.

Delores and Joseph came into the apartment kitchen next.

"Mr. Fairchild!" they both said in surprise, because the owner of the Bessledorf Hotel didn't come to town often. When he did, Mother wanted everything to be perfect.

"I spent an hour at the bus depot just watching the treasure seekers arrive," Mr. Fairchild said. "Such excitement!"

"The town has gone bananas," Delores told him.

"Even the animals know something is up," added Joseph. "I guess it's the sound of all the cars driving in—the starting and stopping and honking—the voices out on the sidewalks. I spent most of my day at the veterinary college tranquilizing the cats and parrots, and calming the dogs."

Mr. Fairchild chuckled some more. "Good! Good!" he said, not seeming to care about the nerves of cats and dogs and parrots.

At that moment Father came into the apartment kitchen and stopped in his tracks. "Mr. Fairchild, sir!" he gasped.

"Ah, don't worry, Theodore, the hotel is in fine shape, I can tell!"

"Shipshape from bow to stern, sir. From mizzen to mast, from starboard to windward, from . . ."

"Muzzle it, Dad," said Delores.

By the time Mother came into the kitchen to start

dinner, and then Lester, it looked like a family council, with Georgene and Weasel there as well. But there was one more tap on the door, and in walked Officer Feeney.

"Could I have a cup of strong coffee, ma'am?" he said to Mother. "I tell you, I haven't seen the likes of this since the ghost appeared at the Bessledorf. Ah, hello there, Mr. Fairchild. Have you come to town with a shovel too?"

"I came to see if the police know anything more about this mysterious stuff than they did before," said Mr. Fairchild.

Feeney sat down at the table with his coffee. "Well, nobody knows for sure, but we're thinking it's all a hoax. We're thinking that the notes have been left in places we're sure to find them, and the message is just difficult enough to sound real, but easy enough to understand."

"But why would anyone go to so much work and trouble, just to trick the town?"

"That's the part we don't know. Somebody with a grudge against that poor old hill, I suspect, the way folks are digging around on it, everyone wanting their piece o' eight."

"Well, if I thought I could carry this on a little longer, I'd go about town leaving messages myself," Mr. Fairchild said. "Let us be in no hurry to solve the case, Feeney. As long as no one is forced to walk the plank, and there are no bodies floating in Middleburg River, what harm are a few holes in the side of a hill?"

"Place is beginning to look like a hunk of Swiss cheese, sir, if you don't mind my saying so," Feeney told him.

"But the holes can be filled up again, Feeney! *Are* being filled up, as fast as they can be dug."

"Of course they are," agreed Theodore, and then, to Officer Feeney, "Don't borrow trouble, officer. If catching a bus to Middleburg adds a bit of excitement to an otherwise dull life, then it is our privilege—nay, our *duty*—to improve the lives of our fellow men. Don't go looking for trouble, lest trouble come looking for you. Don't count your children before they're hatched, or look a gift horse through the nose."

Bernie, Weasel, and Georgene went outside to the alley to let the grown-ups finish their conversation. They climbed up on the wall by the trash cans.

"*I'd* like to find one of those messages the pirates are leaving around," said Georgene. "That would be really exciting, Bernie. How come *we* never see any?"

"I guess the police always find them first," Bernie told her, "but I'm going to keep an eye out for one anyway."

All the way to school and back the next day, Bernie looked everywhere he could think of. He even stuck his hand inside holes in brick walls, searched the weeds along the curb and peeked in trash cans. There were no notes or messages, however, that he could see.

Mr. Fairchild went back to Indianapolis, but every reporter on the newspaper was researching the pirate story, and every day there was another tidbit of information about the history of Middleburg and the pirate Peg Leg, who supposedly sailed up Middleburg River to hide his gold.

The problem was that no one knew anything for sure. The newspaper sent reporters to talk to people who knew people who knew other people who long ago knew the second cousin of the great-grandfather of the sister of Peg Leg's nephew or something, so it was difficult to know what was fact and what was only rumor.

It did seem, however, that until only a few years ago, it was thought that Peg Leg hid his treasure down in the swamps of Louisiana. But no one had ever found it. And recently someone was said to have found a letter that guessed the treasure wasn't in Louisiana at all, but maybe up north in Indiana.

"In Indiana, meaning Middleburg?" Bernie asked his dad.

"Exactly," said his father. "Bernie, my boy, if we were ever lucky enough to find that treasure ourselves, and could keep it, do you know what this would mean?"

"We'd be rich?" Bernie asked.

"We could buy this hotel!" said his father. "*We*, not Mr. Fairchild, would be the owners. *We* would set the rules. *We* would hire the help. *We* would even change the name, from the Bessledorf Hotel to simply *Theodore's*." He leaned back in his chair and looked off into the distance. "I can see the advertisements now: 'Come to Theodore's, where the best rest.'"

Bernie didn't quite see what difference it would make. If they were going to go on living here like this, did it matter whether they were the owners or the managers? Bernie was happy whichever it was.

He was helping Joseph count change at the cash register that night when he looked up suddenly to see a stranger entering the front door of the Bessledorf Hotel.

The man was of medium height, with dark hair, dark eyes, and a black mustache that curled elegantly up at each end. He wore tight black jeans, and a bright red shirt that was unbuttoned halfway down, and there was a thin gold chain about his neck.

He wore no sash, no hat, and no eye patch, but to Bernie, he looked for all the world like a pirate.

Twelve

Delores's Dream

"May I help you?" asked Joseph.

Bernie stared. It was partly the man's mustache and partly the way his eyes looked—as though he could see through Bernie and knew everything he was thinking. But Bernie also couldn't help staring, because the stranger was probably the most handsome man Bernie had seen in his life—more handsome than Joseph, or Bernie's father, even. Bernie just knew that if Delores ever got a look at him, she would . . .

Too late. In walked Delores.

"Joseph," she said, "Mother wants to know if you . . ." And then her eyes fell on the stranger and the stranger's eyes fell on Delores.

"If I what?" asked Joseph.

Delores stood there in a daze. "If you have the

receipts from the cantaloupes in the convertible," she said.

"What?" said Joseph.

"I mean, if you have the refrigerator in the cantaloupes."

"I mean . . ." She gazed even more deeply into the stranger's eyes. "If you have the mustache on the back of the cantaloupes . . ."

"Please excuse my sister," said Bernie. "Since all this pirate business started, she's been a little wacko."

"I understand," said the man with the mustache. "And I would like a room."

"I'm sorry," Joseph told him. "We're completely booked."

"Oh, Joseph, I'm sure we can find a bed for him somewhere!" said Delores. "He can sleep in the kitchen! He can have the bathtub! He can . . ."

"Please, please, I mean to be of no trouble," said the stranger. "But it is important that I stay in Middleburg for at least a week. My name is Raymond Tupper, and I'm the great-great-great-great-great-great-grandson of George Tupper, otherwise known as Peg Leg."

Bernie gasped and Joseph stared, while Delores actually swayed back and forth as though she were about to fall.

"Then *you're* a pirate?" Bernie said.

"No, no, only a distant relative, as you can see."

At that moment the couple in room 117 came down the hall carrying their suitcases.

"Checking out?" Joseph asked, and when they said that they were, Joseph offered Raymond Tupper their room. The man signed the guest register with a flourish, and Delores swayed again, her lips frozen in a wide smile.

The next day was Saturday, and Delores came to breakfast wearing a red ribbon in her hair and a rose pinned to her bosom. She was not wearing the long nightshirt with the picture of Niagara Falls on it that she usually wore at the breakfast table on weekends, but rather she came in a black dress with gold and purple flowers on it, and her nails were painted as red as an apple.

"Are you marching in a parade?" Theodore asked her as she buttered her toast.

"I have reached an age where I am concerned at all times about my appearance," Delores told him. "You never know when I'll meet the man of my dreams."

"In our *kitchen?*" asked Lester, his mouth full of cereal.

"Anywhere," said Delores. "I want to be prepared."

"Love is where you find it," Theodore agreed. "When you go looking for it, it escapes you. The more you give of love, the more you get in return. It is more blessed to give than to receive, and it suffereth long and is kind. It droppeth as the gentle dew from heaven upon the earth beneath, for a rose is a rose is a rose . . ."

"Never mind," said Lester.

Tap, tap, tap . . .

Everyone turned toward the door, and Mother went to open it. There was the stranger with the dark eyes and hair and the mustache that curled up at each end.

Delores was so embarrassed to be caught with a mouth full of toast that she swallowed half a piece, and immediately began to choke.

Her face went from pink to red, and Bernie was alarmed to see it actually turning blue. Delores stumbled up from her chair, her eyes wild and her hands on her throat.

With a leap, the stranger grabbed her from behind and slipped his arms around her waist, hands locked over her stomach. With a quick jab, he pulled his fists inward, and a big wad of toast shot from Delores's mouth, sailed across the kitchen, and hit the door of the refrigerator.

Delores swooned, and the stranger picked her up in his arms.

"You have saved my daughter's life!" cried Mother.

But Delores's eyes remained closed and her arms dangled limply.

The stranger began to look worried. "Perhaps I have not revived her after all," he said.

"She just wants you to do it again," said Lester. Delores's foot shot out and nudged him.

"I'm sure you have done all you possibly can," said Theodore. "If she does not revive by the time I count to ten, sir, I shall take her to the hospital at once to have her stomach pumped."

Delores sat up suddenly, her arms around the stranger's neck. "What happened?" she asked.

"You've been acting like an idiot," Joseph told her.

"I fear I swooned," said Delores.

"Finish your toast, dear," said Mother. "Now, sir, how can we ever repay you?"

"My request is a simple one," said Raymond Tupper, gently lowering Delores to her chair once again. "I wonder where I might find a map of Middleburg. As the great-great-great-great-great-great-grandson of George Tupper, otherwise known as Peg Leg, I feel that if anyone should know where his treasure is buried, I should be that person."

"Absolutely," said Theodore. "Why, we have a map right here in this very hotel! Indeed we do. Please sit down, sir, and I will get one for you."

"Coffee?" said Mother. "Will you have a piece of toast, perhaps, or a muffin?"

"No, thank you," said the man in the red shirt with the thin gold chain about his neck. "I never eat when I work or when I love." And his eyes fell once again on Delores, who was gazing at him in turn, leaning so precariously in his direction, that her arm almost toppled off the table.

Father found the map, and after Raymond Tupper checked his compass and his notebook, he drew a line from the hotel to Bessledorf Hill. Not the near side of the hill, however; not the side that could be seen from the hotel, but the other side, about as far away from town as possible.

"According to my notes," he said, "*that* is where the treasure should be."

Thirteen

His Every Whim

After Raymond Tupper left with his compass, Mr. Magruder called a family conference.

"We have in this hotel a very important person," he said. "It is quite possible that if Mr. Raymond Tupper is fortunate enough to find his great-great-great-great-great-great-grandfather's gold . . ."

"How do you know it's gold?" Lester interrupted.

Mr. Magruder frowned at Lester. "As I was saying, if Mr. Tupper is fortunate enough to find his—"

And the whole family chimed in: "—great-great-great-great-great-great-grandfather's gold—"

"—then it is quite likely," Theodore continued, "quite possible, well . . . conceivable, at least . . . that he might reward the family who made his stay in Middleburg a success."

Delores gave a long, sweet sigh.

"Therefore," said her father, "it is my wish—my *command*, in fact—that you attend to Mr. Tupper's needs."

"Oh, yes!" said Delores.

"His every wish," said Theodore.

"Oh, yes, yes!" said Delores.

"Even a vagrant whim shall not go undetected," continued her father.

"A *what?*" asked Lester.

"He want us to do everything we can to make the guy happy," Bernie translated.

Delores sighed again.

"Lester," said Father. "I want you to find out what Mr. Tupper likes best to eat. Bernie, you find out whether he likes a hard or a soft pillow, one blanket or two. Joseph, you ask if any of our pets disturb him, and Delores, you rush his clothes back and forth to the cleaners, should he ask."

Delores leaned back and closed her eyes, smiling happily.

"While Alma and I," Theodore continued, looking at his wife, "will make sure that any assistance he asks for in finding the treasure will be given."

"What if he finds a chest full of gold and gives us each a dollar?" asked Bernie.

"Then, my boy, we shall simply say that we had the honor of helping the man who is the—"

"—great-great-great-great-great-great-grandson—" the family said.

"—of Peg Leg Tupper find the gold that his great—"

"—great-great-great-great-great-grandfather—" said the family.

"—buried," Theodore finished.

"Amen," said Bernie.

All weekend, the family waited on Raymond Tupper hand and foot. When he walked through the front door in his red shirt with the gold chain around his neck, everyone snapped to attention.

Lester followed him down the hall to his room to ask what he would like for dinner.

"Kidney pie, asparagus soup, and cherries with rum sauce," Mr. Tupper told him.

"Kidney pie, asparagus soup, and cherries with rum sauce it is," said Mother when Lester told her.

Bernie arrived with a pillow under each arm, one soft and one firm, for Mr. Tupper to make a choice, and the man asked if he might also have an extra blanket, preferably wool. Mother rushed right out to buy one.

Joseph held an umbrella over Mr. Tupper when he went out to catch a cab, and was told that the dogs and cats were okay, but that the parrot had awakened him far too early that morning. Joseph assured him that the cover on Salt Water's cage would not be lifted until nine at least.

As for Delores, wherever Raymond Tupper was,

there was Delores also. She brought him an extra cup of coffee at breakfast and sat down to add the sugar.

"Whenever your gorgeous red shirt needs to be cleaned, Mr. Tupper, just tell me," she whispered hoarsely.

"Thank you very much," said Raymond Tupper, gazing back.

"Whenever your tight blue jeans need washing, just whistle," said Delores, leaning closer.

"That's very kind of you," said Raymond Tupper, flashing his gorgeous teeth in a gorgeous smile.

"And when your socks and undies need washing, I shall do them myself with my own two hands," Delores breathed, leaning over so far this time that she knocked over his cup of coffee and had to bring another. This time Raymond Tupper kissed the back of her hand.

"I never saw anything so disgusting in my life," Bernie told his mother. "Are you just going to let her fall all over him like that?"

"She won't fall very far if she keeps falling in his coffee," Mother observed, "but I will indeed speak to her."

At dinner that evening, Mr. Magruder said, "Well, how did things go with Mr. Tupper today?"

"I found out what he likes to eat," said Lester.

"I found out how he likes to sleep," said Bernie.

"I found out how he feels about pets," said Joseph.

Everyone looked at Delores, who was sitting with a dazed look in her eyes and a smile on her lips.

"Delores, my girl?" said Theodore.

"I found out how he likes his undies," said Delores dreamily.

"What?" said her father.

"Theodore, this Tupper man has turned our daughter into a living, breathing, love-sick lunatic," said Mother.

Theodore turned to Delores. "What do you have to say for yourself?" he asked.

Delores continued to smile stupidly and held out her right hand. She pointed to her wrist. "Right there," she said.

"Right there what?" asked Theodore.

"Right there is where he kissed me, and I'll never wash it again. Never."

"She wants to keep somebody's *spit?*" asked Lester.

Mrs. Magruder turned to Delores. "My dear, I agree with you that Raymond Tupper is perhaps the most gorgeous creature on this earth, but we mustn't get carried away now. We mustn't put love before duty. And your duty is to conduct yourself like the fine young woman you are. Be kind to Mr. Tupper, but not *too* kind. In fact, perhaps in the future it would be better if you let the rest of us tend to Mr. Tupper's every whim. Don't you agree, Theodore?"

"Absolutely," said Father. "If you should pass Mr.

Tupper in the lobby again, my girl, you are *not* to gaze into his eyes or fall in his coffee or allow him to kiss your hand. Is that clear? You may say 'Good morning,' but that is all."

Delores only continued smiling.

Theodore reached over and gave her a shake. "Delores, if you meet Mr. Tupper in the lobby, what is it you're going to say?"

Delores looked blankly around the table. "May I wash your undies?" she said.

Fourteen

High and Lively

After Bernie had gone to bed that night, he could hear his parents arguing in the room next to his and Lester's. Bernie never liked to hear his parents quarrel. It made his stomach shrivel, his chest grow cold, his mouth go dry, and his hands sweat, because they didn't quarrel very often, making it all the more scary when they did.

Bernie turned over on his side on the top bunk and put his ear to the wall.

"We'll wake up some morning to find she's run off with that man!" Mother was saying.

"Would that be so bad?" Father said.

"Theodore!" Bernie heard his mother say on the other side of the wall. "Have you no shame? Our daughter run off with a *pirate?*"

"The great-great-great—"

"—great-great-great—" whispered Bernie.

"—grandson of a pirate," Theodore finished. "Would that be so bad?"

"Well, *I* think we should put a stop to things right now," said Mother. "Lock the girl up, if necessary."

"Now, now, let's don't be hasty," said Father. "If Raymond Tupper *were* to find that treasure, he could make our daughter a very wealthy woman indeed."

"Is that all you care about?" asked Mother, and Bernie thought she was crying now. Then he realized that the sniffles came from the bunk just below him.

"Bernie?" said Lester. "Do you think they'll get a divorce?"

"Of course not. All parents argue now and then," Bernie told him.

"If they do split, who gets the dog?" Lester asked, still sniffling.

"They're just arguing about Delores, that's all—the way she's been carrying on about Raymond Tupper."

The bedroom was quiet for a few minutes. There was a murmur from their parents' bedroom occasionally, but no one was shouting now.

"Why don't we just get rid of her," came Lester's voice at last.

"What?" cried Bernie. "Who?"

"Delores. If Mom and Dad are going to fight about her, let's just get rid of her."

"Lester!"

"If Raymond Tupper finds a chest of gold, we'll ask him how much he'd pay to take Delores with him."

"Sell her?"

"She'd be worth a lot. She's got gold fillings in her teeth," said Lester.

"I can't believe you're saying this," Bernie told him. He thought it over. "Besides, what if Raymond Tupper didn't want her?"

"Then we could put an ad in the paper," Lester told him. "In the give-away column, where they advertise dogs and cats."

"Forget it, Lester. Mom and Dad will stop quarreling when Delores turns normal again, and Delores will be normal again when Raymond Tupper rides off into the sunset. He's not about to ride off until he finds the treasure, though, so we've got to help all we can."

Maybe the thing to do, he was thinking, was try to find out from Raymond Tupper just how he honestly felt about Delores. Then, if he said he really loved her, Bernie would ask him if he couldn't marry her and get her out of the house as soon as possible.

There could be a grand wedding right there at the Bessledorf Hotel, with Delores floating down the same big staircase on which they'd seen the ghost, with the minister and Raymond Tupper waiting for her at the bottom.

The minister would say, "Do you, Delores, take this man, the great-great-great-great-great-great-grandson of Peg Leg the Pirate, to be your lawful wedded husband?"

And after Delores said yes, the minister would say, "Do you, the great-great-great-great-great-great-grandson of Peg Leg the Pirate, take Delores to be your lawful wedded wife?" And all the Magruders, he knew, would be whispering, "Take her! Take her! Take her!"

Bernie was at the registration desk the following morning when two painters arrived in their overalls and paint caps. Mother was writing the next chapter of *The Passionate Pocketbook* in the apartment behind the registration desk, so Bernie was out front answering the phone.

"Good morning," said one of the painters. "We're here to start the painting."

"The painting?" asked Bernie.

The man reached in his pocket and pulled out a letter, handing it to Bernie.

Dear Theodore:
Two banker friends of mine are coming to Middleburg soon. They've heard about the treasure on Bessledorf Hill and want to be in on the excitement. Their names are Dan Lively and Rutherford High, and they'll be traveling with their wives. Their

visit is *very* important to me, Theodore, and I want to impress this on you and your family. If they enjoy their stay at the Bessledorf, they may well invest in our hotel and make it the finest hotel in the state of Indiana. For this reason I am completely redecorating rooms 309 and 311, and these painters know what to do. At the same time, I want no one to know that the bankers are in town, for I do not want other businesses trying to woo them for their money. Do not mention their names, not even to me if I call. If things are going well with the redecorating, all you need say is, "We're stepping high and lively, sir." If they are not, say, "We're not stepping quite so high and lively, sir." That's all. You'll need to vacate rooms 309 and 311, of course, but let me assure you, it will be worth it.

L. Fairchild

"Um . . . just a minute," Bernie said when he'd read the letter, and he took it to his father, who was instructing Mrs. Verona about dinner.

Mr. Magruder read the letter and his eyes opened wide. Without a word to Mrs. Verona, he went out into the lobby.

"Bring in your buckets and ladders, by all means," he told the painters. "It may take some time, but I will vacate the rooms for you." And then, to Bernie, he smiled and said, "This could be the start of something big!"

The people in rooms 309 and 311, of course, didn't think so.

"What do you mean, I've got to move?" asked the man in 309, when Mr. Magruder called him on the phone. Bernie could hear him yelling through the receiver.

"I'm sorry, sir, but there seems to be a problem with the walls, and it's for your own safety. We have a room vacating on the first floor, and we'll be glad to move you there. I'm very sorry for the inconvenience," Theodore told him.

The man grumbled some more, but he allowed Bernie to help him move.

The people in 311 were *very* upset. "No, we don't want to move!" they said. "We have a reservation for three nights, and we've only been here one. Either we stay in this room three nights or we're not paying for any of them."

"Then I'm afraid you'll not pay for any, sir, because I have to move you out," Mr. Magruder said.

Finally the rooms were empty, the beds and dressers and chairs covered with painters' cloths, and the painting began.

"What are the painters doing on third?" asked Mother as she noticed the men going in and out in their white caps and overalls.

"Just a little project for Mr. Fairchild," Theodore told her, winking at Bernie, and Bernie winked back.

"Who's redecorating?" Delores asked at dinner. "If there's any wallpapering to be done, they can start on my room. I'm sick of looking at birds and marsh grass. Whoever wallpapered my room must have lived in a swamp."

"When this is over, we may be able to redecorate the whole hotel," Mr. Magruder declared secretively. And when the family looked at him curiously, he said to Delores, "What kind of wallpaper would you prefer, my dear?"

"Hearts and flowers," Delores said dreamily. It was then Bernie noticed the gardenia in her hair.

"Who sent the flower?" he asked.

"Someone with a red shirt and tight jeans and a black mustache and a gold chain around his handsome neck," said Delores. "The man of my dreams, the hope of my life."

Mr. and Mrs. Magruder exchanged worried glances.

At that moment the phone rang and Theodore answered.

"Mr. Fairchild!" he said. "Yes, indeed sir, everything is going well. Going splendidly, in fact. We are stepping high and lively, sir. High and lively indeed!"

Fifteen

Keeping the Secret

"What's going on at the Bessledorf?" Weasel asked when he and Georgene came over later that week to practice blowing bubblegum bubbles in the alley. Weasel still thought he might get his name in the *Guinness Book of World Records* for the largest bubble ever blown.

"The usual," said Bernie. "People coming and going, everyone looking for treasure but nobody finding any."

"What are you having painted?" asked Georgene. "I saw some painters going in and out."

Bernie *almost* told her about Mr. Lively and Mr. High, but stopped himself in time.

"Bernie, my boy," his father had told him again that morning. "This is a secret between the two of us, and not even you would know it if you hadn't read Mr. Fairchild's letter. No one, not even your mother, is to know of the two bankers coming to our hotel."

"Not even *Mom?*" Bernie had asked, surprised.

"Your mother is a wonderful woman, Bernie," his father had told him. "The salt of the earth, the apple of my eye, the fruit of the tree, and the fire of my soul, but she *does* like to talk, and talk *does* get around. This has got to be a secret between you and me and Mr. Fairchild. Understand?"

"Yes, sir," Bernie had said, feeling very important.

"You know what I think?" said Georgene, as they watched the bubble at Weasel's lips grow larger and larger until it almost hid his nose. "I think that if there *was* any treasure on Bessledorf Hill, it's been found by now."

Pop! The bubblegum bubble lay plastered over Weasel's chin.

"Huh-uh," said Weasel, shoving the gum back in his mouth again. "Officer Feeney said they're still finding notes around town."

"I'll bet that's just to throw people off guard," said Georgene. "Whoever found that treasure is probably in Mexico right now, living it up. What would *you* do if you found a chest of gold, Bernie?"

Bernie had to think about that. His first thought was to buy a new skateboard with blue and silver stripes. He had even seen some in catalogs that had small lights on both ends so that when he did tricks on his skateboard at night, it would make designs in the dark. But a chest of gold would buy hundreds and thousands of skateboards, perhaps, so the next thing he would buy was a bike, and maybe some high-top sneakers with black and gold laces. And after that he'd give every member of his family some of the money, and after that . . . Well, maybe, he'd just take it down to the bus depot and give it away to the poor.

"I'd buy a boat," said Georgene. "If I had a chest of gold, I would buy a boat that would go either by motor or by sail, and I'd take it on all the rivers of the world. I'd go scuba diving off the coast of Florida and fishing in California and I'd go all the way to Alaska and back. What would *you* do, Weasel?"

Weasel thought and thought. "I guess I'd give it to my grandfather to buy some new teeth," he said.

"What?" cried Bernie.

"Teeth." Weasel nodded. "So he could eat corn on the cob in summer and apples in the fall, and I wouldn't have to listen to him complain anymore. Then maybe I'd buy myself a lifetime supply of Milky Way bars."

The three sat watching the fireflies and thinking about what they would do if they were rich, and Bernie was just about to suggest that a chest of gold would probably buy a fine home in the country with a lake and horses to ride, when they heard voices coming from the garden. There were footsteps and then the sound of someone sitting in the two-seater swing among the rose bushes.

"Delores, my dove," came a voice which Bernie recognized as Raymond Tupper's. "I cannot tell you what your friendship has meant to me these last few days."

"Oh, Raymond!" sighed Delores.

"Without your faith in me, I'm not sure I could go on. Searching, searching, always searching . . . I have always known that somewhere, sometime, I would discover where my great-great-great-great-great-great-grandfather buried his treasure, and now that I know, or *think* I know, I am determined that nothing shall stop me, and I will, at last, obtain what rightly belongs to me."

"Oh, Raymond!" Delores sighed again.

"With you by my side, nothing can stop me. I *will* succeed, my darling, and you shall share my prize."

"Oh, Raymond!"

Bernie nudged Georgene on one side of him and Weasel on the other, and they nudged back.

"Delores, my life, my love, I have a question I want to ask you," Raymond Tupper continued.

"Yes? Yes?" cried Delores.

Raymond cleared his throat. "As the great-great-great-great-great-great-grandson of Peg Leg, if I *do* find my great-great—"

"Oh, never mind the greats, what's the question?" asked Delores.

"If I *do* find the treasure, will you—"

"Yes, yes, yes, yes, yes, yes, yes!" answered Delores.

"—will you keep the secret of where it was buried?" finished Raymond Tupper.

"*What?*" said Delores.

"The secret. Everyone seems to think that the treasure is buried on the near side of Bessledorf Hill, while my compass shows me precisely that it is on the far side."

"*That's* the question you wanted to ask?" cried Delores, her voice heavy with disappointment. "What difference does it make *where* it was buried, once it's found?"

"Just in case there is more, and I have to go digging again. We can let *no* one know where I find it, until we are safely out of town."

"*We?*" cried Delores, sounding hopeful again.

"Yes, we," said Raymond. "And then I shall ask you a question of a different sort."

"Oh, Raymond!" sighed Delores. "And the answer shall be yes, a thousand times yes, and I shall be happy washing your socks for the rest of my life!"

Georgene nudged Bernie again and so did Weasel, and Bernie could feel them shaking with laughter. He almost laughed out loud himself.

He wished, however, that Raymond Tupper had told her before to keep the secret. Because, since the day in the kitchen when Raymond Tupper had taken out his compass and map and decided that the treasure was on the far side of Bessledorf Hill, Bernie had told Georgene and Weasel, and Joseph had told his friends at the veterinary college, and Delores had told the girls at the parachute factory. Bernie was sure that at least fifty people now suspected that the gold was not where most of the treasure hunters were digging at all. Raymond Tupper might be the great-great-great-great-great-great-grandson of Peg Leg Tupper, but he wasn't very bright, Bernie concluded.

But Bernie still hoped that the man in the tight black jeans and the bright red shirt would find the treasure, that he would marry Delores, and take her as far away from Middleburg as they could get. If he saw his sister maybe once a year, Bernie figured, that would be about right.

Sixteen

In Code

Bernie almost hated to go to school every morning because he did not know what he might miss while he was gone. At school it was the same old thing—fractions and spelling and band and geography, but as soon as he started home, he saw throngs of people heading toward Bessledorf Hill with their shovels, and hordes of people coming back. The buses came and went, with people who had already dug and were disappointed and with people who figured they could find at least one spot on Bessledorf Hill where nobody else had thought to dig.

"Don't worry," the mayor said, when residents complained that there wasn't a blade of grass left on the hill. "This will blow over by and by, and we'll plant the whole hill in grass."

Each day, however, it seemed as though there were fewer and fewer people on the near side of Bessledorf Hill, and more and more people on the far side. Raymond Tupper's secret hadn't stayed secret very long. Nevertheless, the great-great-great-great-great-great-grandson of Peg Leg Tupper remained cheerful. He waited until all the other treasure seekers had quit for the day and come back to the Bessledorf to clean up and enjoy a good dinner. Then, while they were sitting around in the lobby afterward playing cards, Raymond Tupper crept over to Bessledorf Hill and did his digging in the dark.

And always, before he left, he gave Delores a long, sweet kiss by the back door.

"Be careful, my love," she told him.

"I will, my dove," he answered.

Bernie did not understand about love. What he did understand, however, was that everybody seemed to be living an exciting life except him. At the bus station, people were coming and going. At the hotel, people were checking in and out. On the third floor, the painters were bringing in rolls of wallpaper, and strips of molding, and buckets of paint, and sacks of powdered plaster. But Bernie's life was the same as always. It looked as though everyone else might be on the verge of becoming rich, but not Bernie.

Not only was Bernie feeling not at all rich, but he was feeling unusually poor. He had not been careful with his allowance. He had spent it on a movie with Georgene and Weasel (*The Revenge of the Creepy Crawlers*), bought a double chocolate malted afterward, and then a couple of comic books on the way home. Now, when he needed a new notebook for science class, he had only fifty cents left.

When Bernie needed money, there were three possibilities:

1. Earn it, which meant asking his parents what jobs needed doing. The jobs they suggested were never the *fun* jobs, however, but rather the weeding of the garden or the scrubbing of the toilets or something, so this was never Bernie's first choice.

2. Find it. Sometimes, if Bernie walked all the way to school and back with his eyes on the ground, he would find a penny or nickel or even a dime or quarter. And there was always the possibility of finding it in the pockets of his jeans or, failing that, between the sofa cushions, but it didn't happen very often.

3. Go without.

And so, on this particular day, Bernie took all his pants and jackets from the closet and shook them upside down over his bed. He found a penny in his jeans and a nickel in his jacket, but that was all.

Next he went into the lobby to check between the couch cushions, and was disappointed to find Felicity Jones sitting at one end of the sofa and Mrs. Buzzwell at the other, along with Mr. Lamkin, who sat in the middle, all watching the soap opera *No Tomorrow* on TV. Bernie had to sit down and watch it with them so that as soon as they left, he could check the cushions before anyone else sat there.

On the screen, a woman with long blond hair had just thrown her arms around a man with a black mustache.

"Oh, please don't leave me!" she begged.

"I must go, my darling, never to return," said the man, gently removing her arms from around his neck.

"But I shall die without you!" the woman cried, and Bernie heard a sob from Felicity Jones and Mrs. Buzzwell.

"Then I shall have to live with that, a weight upon my heart," the man told her. "Farewell."

And even Mr. Lamkin swallowed.

Bernie wondered if that's the way things would end between Delores and the pirate—the great-great-great-great-great-great-grandson of a pirate, that is. He had heard Mother talk of women who had "taken to their beds," never to go out again, and wondered what life would be like here at the Bessledorf if that should happen to Delores.

At last the program was over. Felicity went off to

her room to cry, Mr. Lamkin went out for a walk, and Mrs. Buzzwell went to the hotel dining room to fortify herself with a butterscotch sundae.

As soon as they were gone, Bernie lifted up the sofa cushions. There was a gum wrapper, a comb, a penny, and a ballpoint pen.

He sat on one end of the sofa and slid his hand down between the side of the couch and the cushion. Slowly his fingers moved along the narrow space, searching for the feel of a smooth coin. Yes! A quarter! *Two* quarters, in fact! Bernie could not believe how lucky he was. Eagerly he searched for more, and his fingers closed at last upon what felt like a dollar bill. He pulled it out.

It was not a dollar bill. It was a folded piece of paper on which the initials *J.L.* were written.

Bernie sat staring at the paper a long time. It was not a note for him, he knew. But he did not know any J.L., either. The only person he knew of in the hotel whose last name began with *L* was Mr. Lamkin, and *his* first name was Samuel. And who knew how old the note was? It could have been there for many years, and Bernie was just now finding it.

Slowly his fingers unfolded it and spread it out in his lap.

J.L., the message read. *S.W. 9. N.L.—P.*

Seventeen

Juicy Lambchop

Bernie could scarcely believe his eyes. A message. A message in code! And *he* had found it. He had found it not stuck in the gate of the funeral parlor or between two bricks in an alley, but hidden where almost no one else in Middleburg would have thought to look.

His heart pounded hard in his chest. Should he give it to his dad? Show it to his mom? At the same time he thought it, he knew what he was going to do: show it to Georgene and Weasel. *Finders keepers!*

"O.T.," he whispered to them as they went inside the school building the next morning, and at recess, when they met under the oak tree, he slipped the note out of his pocket and showed it to them.

"Wow!" breathed Weasel.

"Do you have any idea what it means?" Georgene asked.

"Not the slightest. Come over after school and we'll see if we can figure it out."

The day could not go fast enough. Bernie gulped down his lunch as though that would bring on the afternoon sooner, and he handed in his arithmetic paper before anyone else, then sat looking at the clock, wondering why the hands weren't moving.

"Bernie," said their teacher. "Slow down. All day you've been acting like a racehorse at the starting gate. If it *was* three o'clock, what would you be doing that's so important?"

And before Bernie could think, he heard himself saying, "Digging for treasure." Everyone laughed.

"Well, let's dig a little harder on these math problems," the teacher said, handing his paper back. "I've counted two wrong in the first row already."

At last the bell rang and Bernie was first out the door, Georgene and Weasel close at his heels. Soon they were sitting on the top bunk in Bernie's bedroom, a plate of graham crackers in front of them with a chair braced against the door so Lester couldn't get in.

They stared at the note Bernie had found: *J.L.*, *S.W. 9. N.L.—P.*

"Well, for starters, let's guess that J.L. is the person who's getting the note, and P. is the one who wrote it, and see if it makes any sense," Georgene suggested.

Bernie told them how he didn't know anyone in the hotel with those initials. In fact, he had even checked the guest list at the registration desk.

"A few *J*s for first names and a couple *L*s for the last, but nobody with both a *J* and an *L*."

They studied it some more. "*S.W.* probably stands for southwest," said Weasel. "But then what does *N.L.* mean?"

They tried to think of everything else *S.W.* and *N.L.* might stand for.

"So what; never late," guessed Georgene.

"Soaking wet; need Levis," guessed Weasel.

"Skinny worms; mostly leeches," said Bernie.

They weren't getting very far.

Suddenly Georgene had an idea. "Maybe it's a love note in code from Raymond Tupper to Delores!"

Bernie felt his heart sink. *That* was no fun!

Weasel made a face. "*She's* not J.L., and he's not P."

"But maybe they have secret names for each other," Georgene insisted. "It could be 'Juicy Lambchop, from Peachy.' "

"Then what would the rest mean?" asked Weasel. For a long time there was no sound but the munching of graham crackers.

"Hey, Bernie, what are you guys doing in there?" came Lester's voice. "Let me in."

"We're having a secret conference," Bernie called back.

"Well, it's my room too!"

"In a minute!" Bernie yelled.

"Who's got the graham crackers?"

Bernie sighed and got down off the bed. He opened the door and gave the box to Lester, then closed it again.

"Okay, I've got it," said Georgene. "How's this? 'Juicy Lambchop. Some Wednesday, 9 o'clock. No luggage. Peachy.'"

"Meaning?"

"That they plan to elope some Wednesday at nine, and they won't bring any suitcases so no one will get suspicious," said Georgene.

Bernie's heart began to thump. Maybe this note was more important than he thought. What if Georgene was right? Should he tell his parents? Or should he just hope Delores would be happy ever after, and then he could have her room?

Why tell his parents? Wasn't Delores a grown woman? Wasn't she entitled to happiness with the man of her dreams?

"I think you're right," he said. "What do we do now?"

"We have to make sure," said Georgene. "If it *is* a love note from Raymond Tupper to Delores, she'll probably send him one in reply, and she'll probably hide it in the same place."

"How can she reply when she doesn't even know about this one?" asked Weasel.

"That's right!" said Georgene. "If we've got the note, nobody else will see it."

So Bernie copied the message down on the back of his school notebook, and later that afternoon, he went into the lobby again to put the message back.

Eighteen

Making a Scene

It was almost more excitement than Bernie could take. A real live message, found by *him*, and nobody else in the hotel knew about it. Of course, the message could be a year old. It might be the measurements for a rug or something that just dropped out of someone's pocket and wasn't supposed to be secret at all. It was the chance he would have to take.

The problem was getting the message back where he had found it without anyone noticing. To make matters worse, Mother had decided that Hildegarde, the cleaning woman, should remove all the cushions off all the chairs and sofas in the lobby and vacuum them well. Bernie swallowed when he saw how easily the message might have been discovered by someone else, as Hildegarde thrust the nozzle of the vacuum cleaner down between the cushions and the side of the couch.

After the red-haired Hildegarde finished vacuuming and left the lobby, Bernie was just about to put the message back when Mr. Wilkins, the handyman, came in to wash the windows. Bernie didn't think he could stand it. He spent the time trying to teach Salt Water to say, "Avast, ye swabs!" but when the parrot said it, it sounded more like, "Wash your scabs," and Mother said that was disgusting.

While he waited, Bernie took Mixed Blessing for a walk. The Great Dane loved being outdoors and was so large that people always stopped to stare. Mother felt safe with the big dog in the hotel. She said she didn't think she need worry too much about robbers with Mixed Blessing about.

Officer Feeney was out walking his beat, and Mixed Blessing, taking off after a squirrel, almost knocked the policeman down.

"Danged dog!" Feeney complained, picking up his hat. "Dog that big should have headlights and a horn so you can see him coming."

"Sorry," said Bernie. "He's just trying to be friendly. Any news about the treasure?"

"Treasure, schmeasure!" said Feeney. "I wish this town had never heard of Peg Leg. So many people taking a shovel to that hill we might just as well dig up the hill ourselves, parcel it out in Jiffy bags, and sell the dirt for a dollar apiece. That's all folks are going away with anyhow—dirt."

"And nobody's found a thing?"

"Not a penny," said Feeney. "Even the messages left about town have stopped. If you ask me, whoever came to get that gold got what he was after and is gone again."

Hearing that, Bernie was more excited still. The messages had *not* stopped coming!

He took Mixed Blessing back home again, fed Lewis and Clark, who were meowing for supper, checked in a supply of fresh sheets and towels that had arrived at the front desk from the laundry, and told Joseph to go rest, that he'd take over the registration desk for a while.

"Thanks, Bernie, I'm really tired," Joseph told him. "Somebody had his pet poodle out with him while he was traipsing all over Bessledorf Hill, looking for gold, and the poor little dog was exhausted. I had to push fluids on him all day. Then there was another dog whose owner took him with her while she was digging for gold. She accidentally stepped in the hole she was digging and fell on top of her dog. If this pirate thing doesn't end soon, we're going to have half the animals in Middleburg in the clinic."

He slung his suit coat over his shoulder and went back in the hotel apartment to rest. At long last, Bernie was alone in the lobby.

He got up and walked around the registration desk,

across the carpet, past Salt Water's perch, and had just reached in his pocket for the message when a high voice cackled, "Avast, ye swabs!"

Bernie jumped a foot. "Salt Water!" he said with relief. "You finally got it right!" And then, before anything else could happen, he thrust his hand down between the side of the sofa and the cushion, and left the little piece of paper right where he'd found it.

"Did you do it?" Weasel asked him the next day at school.

Bernie nodded.

"Have you looked yet to see if anyone took it?" asked Georgene.

"I didn't have a chance. Every time I go to the lobby, someone's there. I'll check tonight for sure."

To help, Georgene and Weasel went home with Bernie that day.

"We'll make sure nobody looks at you when you see if the message is gone," Georgene said.

"What are you going to do? Set off tear gas?" Bernie joked.

"You'll see," Georgene told him.

They walked into the hotel. There were people all around. No one happened to be watching television, but some were playing cards in one corner, some were at the registration desk waiting for a room, some were going into the hotel restaurant, and some were coming out. The cats, Lewis and Clark, were sitting on either end of the mantel, and Mixed Blessing was running around in a circle because Lester had just given him the crust off his peanut butter and banana sandwich, and was ready to take him for a walk.

"All these people!" cried Bernie. "I'll never get a chance to see if the note's still there. It's hopeless!"

"No it's not," said Georgene. "Watch me, and as soon as you see your chance, go for it."

She stepped out into the center of the lobby and suddenly fell to the floor, one hand clutching her ankle. "Ow! Ow! Ow!" she cried.

Instantly all talking stopped and all faces turned in her direction. Everybody who was sitting on the couch stood up to see what was happening, and three of the men rushed forward to help.

In that split second, Bernie sat down at one end of the sofa, thrust his hand deep down between the cushion and the side of the couch. Something was there. It was not the little folded piece of paper he had left the night before, but a small rolled-up sheet of paper instead. He swiftly took it out and thrust it in his pocket, then sauntered over to where Mr. Magruder and the bellhop were helping Georgene to her feet.

"I guess I just sort of turned my ankle," said Georgene, her voice weak and trembly. "Thank you." She limped on over to Bernie and Weasel and then, draping an arm around each of their shoulders, hobbled slowly out the back door of the hotel.

Nineteen

Peachy

"Was it there?" Georgene asked, as soon as they were out the door.

"Something was," said Bernie.

They climbed up on the wall beyond the garden, and Bernie took the paper out of his pocket. This time it was yellow.

"A new note!" whispered Georgene. "Open it quick!"

Eagerly Bernie unfolded the small sheet of note paper, and then his heart beat double time. Another message in code: *P—K.T.!—J.L.*

Now they knew for sure that J.L. and P. were persons, and that they were sending notes back and forth. Bernie had goose bumps on his arms.

"Wow, Bernie, this is really spooky," breathed Georgene. "We're on to something, all right."

"Unless it's another lovey-dovey note between Delores and Raymond Tupper," said Weasel.

"Oh. Right. I forgot," said Georgene, sounding disappointed herself.

They tried their best to see if they couldn't make some kind of pirate message out of it.

"Maybe it's, 'Pirates, kill town!'" said Bernie at last.

"'Pirates, kill Tupper!' How about that?" asked Weasel.

"Or 'Pirates, kill tomorrow,'" offered Georgene. They were quiet awhile, studying the note some more. Finally Georgene sighed. "But what is it most *likely* to be?" she asked.

"A note from Juicy Lambchop to Peachy," said Bernie, some of the excitement gone.

Georgene nodded. "'Peachy,'" she suggested. "'Kissy-tum. Juicy Lambchop.'"

"That's stretching it," said Bernie. "I don't think so."

He held the paper to his nose and took a long breath to see if he could detect Delores's perfume.

"You know," he said. "Maybe we were right to begin with. Maybe that first note *did* mean that something is going to happen at nine tomorrow—that Delores and Raymond Tupper are going to run away together."

"Morning or evening?" asked Weasel.

"I don't know," said Bernie.

"Then you'd better tell your parents," Georgene said. "They might want to stop her."

Then again, they might not, Bernie decided.

"Maybe that first note meant that something is going to happen at nine tomorrow or the next day. Maybe Delores and Raymond Tupper are going to run away together at nine in the evening."

"That's it, Bernie! I'll bet that's what all this means," said Georgene. "Are you going to tell your folks?"

"I've got to think about it some more. We're not really sure of anything, you know," Bernie said.

His friends went home at five thirty, and at six, the whole family sat down to dinner in the kitchen of their apartment. Bernie decided that he would wait and see if Delores would tell the family herself that she was going off with the great-great-great-great-great-great-grandson of Peg Leg Tupper. If so, he wouldn't say a word about finding her note.

Forks clinked against plates and knives against spoons, as Joseph told about a cat that almost lost its tail and Mother said, "*Joseph*, not at the table!"

Then Lester complained because his lunch sack that day had contained a salami sandwich when he had clearly asked for peanut butter and banana, and Delores said could everyone just be quiet for a change, she was trying to think.

Aha! thought Bernie.

The Magruders managed to stay quiet for all of thirty seconds, and finally Theodore looked at his daughter and said, "Silence is golden, my dear, but unburdening your heart to your family is noble indeed."

"Ha!" said Delores, and noisily bit into a carrot.

"He's right," said Mother. "Many a night your father and I have not felt like speaking to each other, but before we go to sleep we always talk it out and never go to sleep without a kiss. Why don't you try it?"

"Ha!" said Delores again. "I'm not kissing anybody, unless . . ." And then she got that faraway look in her eyes again.

Mr. and Mrs. Magruder exchanged glances.

"Delores, I am going to come right out and ask you," Theodore said, putting down his fork. "Are you or are you not seeing Raymond Tupper on the sly?"

"What does *that* mean?" Delores asked.

"I mean without our knowing about it."

"Of course! I see him here. I see him there. I see all the guests coming or going, and I don't tell you when I look at them and when I don't."

"But are you . . . you're not . . . would you consider . . .?" stammered Mother.

"Marrying him?" Bernie finished.

"If she does, can I have her room?" asked Lester, and Bernie kicked him under the table. If *any*body was getting Delores's room, it would be him.

"Don't be silly," said Delores, picking up her carrot again, but that was neither a yes or no. So when dinner was over, Bernie followed her down the hall to her room. She was about to close the door when she saw him there in the doorway.

"What do *you* want?" she demanded.

"Listen, Delores, I just think you ought to know that I know who Lambchop and Peachy are," he said.

"What?" Delores looked at him as though he were crazy.

"And I know that *something* is going to happen at nine o'clock, don't think I don't."

"Well, if something happens at nine o'clock, please tell me about it, because I'll be right here in my room," Delores told him, and shut her door.

Now what? Bernie wondered. Maybe he'd struck out. He had to admit that Delores seemed not to know what he was talking about. Maybe the note wasn't for her. Maybe it had nothing to do with Delores. Maybe it really *was* pirate talk, and he and Georgene and Weasel just didn't know it.

He could hardly sleep that night because the mystery rolled around and around in his head. He tried to think of everything that K.T. and J.L. and P. could mean. It just didn't make a lot of sense.

He turned first one way, then another. The moon sailed on by one window and shone in another. Out in the hallway, Mixed Blessing snored. The clock in the hallway chimed two and, after a long while, three. Bernie was almost ready to turn on his bed light and read for a while when he heard a soft *tap, tap, tap*. He lifted his head off the pillow and listened. *Tap, tap, tap*, the noise came again.

It was not Lewis or Clark scratching to get in, that he was sure of. It was not a limb scraping against his window, because there were no trees outside the window. It was not the furnace or refrigerator.

Tap, tap, tap, the sound continued.

Slowly, softly, Bernie got out of bed.

Twenty

———

Call from Fairchild

Tap.

Tap, tap.

One if by land, and two if by sea, Bernie thought.
Was someone sending signals?

When he got out in the lobby, he stood very still.
He could hear Mixed Blessing snoring over by the
door. He could just make out the two cats asleep on
the couch, and the silhouette of Salt Water's perch
there in front of the window.

Tap . . . tap . . . tap . . .

The noise seemed to come from upstairs.

Slowly, slowly, step by step, Bernie started up the stairs.
He did not want to take the elevator because he was
afraid he would lose the sound. It was a soft, timid sound—
like someone not wanting to make too much noise.

Slowly, slowly, step by step, Bernie turned on the landing and went up the stairs to second. Then he made his way to third.

He stopped and listened some more. For a long time all was quiet. Maybe it had been the wind, blowing something against the building. A branch, perhaps. But then the noise came again.

Slowly, slowly, step by step, Bernie started down the long carpeted hall of the third floor.

Creak, went the floorboards beneath his feet, and he stopped. Someone would know he was coming.

He noticed a light from under a doorway halfway down the hall—just a pale, yellow light. He wouldn't knock on that door no matter what. He and Lester and Joseph and Delores had been told they must never, ever knock on a guest room door of the Bessledorf unless they had a message to deliver or the hotel was on fire, one or the other.

Bernie decided that if he just stood outside the door, he could tell if the tapping had been coming from the room with the pale, yellow light shining under the door. And if the door ever opened, then Bernie could ask if anything was the matter.

So he sat down cross-legged in the hall, facing the door, back to the wall, and waited. Nothing happened, however, and after awhile he closed his eyes. He sat and sat and waited and waited, and the next thing he knew, he heard a door click.

He struggled to open his eyes, to figure out where he was. He knew he was not in bed, but pieces of a dream floated about in his head, along with a vague memory of coming upstairs, and by the time he was awake enough to open his eyes, the person had disappeared down the stairs, the light had gone out under the guest room door, and when Bernie got down to the lobby and found it empty, he realized with dismay that he had even failed to notice what room it was that he had been waiting outside. He had found out nothing. Absolutely nothing.

The next day there was excitement all over town. A message had been found between two fingers of the statue outside city hall. The bronze general was standing there with a pigeon atop his head, a plumber reported, and a piece of paper stuck between two fingers of his right hand. The plumber, being curious, just had to see what the paper said.

As soon as he'd read it, he took it right to the newspaper, which printed it on page one: *J.L. Pay dirt! N.W. side—15 p. from wall. Lots left. Help me dig.*

Bernie stared at the newspaper. As anyone could plainly tell, it said that someone had found a treasure fifteen paces from the wall on the northwest side of Bessledorf Hill, and that a lot of gold was left. So much, in fact, that help was needed in the digging.

All the officers on Middleburg's police force were placed on duty to control the crowds. Some treasure seekers were so eager to dig that they whacked each other with their shovels, wanting to get there first.

Police had to be on guard all night, not only on Bessledorf Hill itself, but stationed at every block along the street heading up the hill.

"You see?" said Felicity Jones to Mr. Magruder as she passed him in the hotel lobby. "I *told* you there was something going on up on that hill. I *told* you I saw a yellow bobbing light."

"Indeed you did," said Father. "I only wish we knew what it meant and who was doing the bobbing."

"I wonder when Mr. Fairchild's banker friends will be coming to town to join in the treasure hunt," mused Mrs. Magruder at dinner that evening. "They should have been here by now."

Bernie and his father stared at each other.

"How did you know about the banker friends?" asked Mr. Magruder. "That was supposed to be secret."

"Theodore, my dear, my love, if you want to keep something secret you don't go leaving letters about," said Mother. "You left that letter right on top of our dresser, and I have told the entire staff to treat the bankers well when they arrive."

Mr. Magruder groaned.

"If they don't come pretty soon, the treasure will be gone," said Joseph.

"If there *is* a treasure," said Delores. "If you ask me, this whole town's gone nuts."

"The painters have assured me they are about done," said Mr. Magruder, "but I'll check on them tomorrow. There is no point in telling you all to keep this secret, I suppose, because you have probably already told your friends."

"I haven't," said Bernie.

Theodore looked proudly down the table at Bernie. "My boy, you are a Magruder through and through," he said. "Keeping a confidence is akin to godliness, for where your treasure is, there will your heart be also."

"What did he say?" asked Lester.

"That it's good to keep your promise," said Bernie.

The phone rang just then, and Delores stopped chewing her celery stalk long enough to answer: "Pirate's Treasure Crazy House," she said.

"Delores!" chided her father.

And then Delores turned pink, for the whole family could hear Mr. Fairchild's voice on the end of the line.

Father grabbed the phone away from Delores. "Sir?" he said.

"Crazy house or not, Theodore, this treasure thing is bringing business to Middleburg, and money to my hotel," said Mr. Fairchild, loud enough for the whole family to hear.

"We're stepping high and lively, sir," said Theodore.

"Well, that's good to hear. Are all my rooms filled?"

"We're stepping high and lively, sir," said Theodore again.

"Good, good. Are the rooms kept clean and bright, with every convenience provided?"

"We're stepping high and lively, sir," Mr. Magruder reported.

"Theodore, you stupid idiot! Can't you say anything else?" Fairchild bellowed. "You keep those rumors going now, and let's hope that the treasure, if there *is* a treasure, won't be found for a long, long time."

"He never called me an idiot before," Theodore said as he hung up the phone, puzzled.

Why, wondered Bernie, would Mr. Fairchild get angry when his father was merely following instructions with all that "high and lively" business?

"You know what?" said Joseph. "It wouldn't surprise me if Mr. Fairchild started the rumors about a treasure himself, and if it wasn't *him* coming down from Indianapolis in the dead of night, leaving notes all around town, just to bring in busloads of treasure seekers and business to his hotel."

"Why, Joseph, what an idea!" said his father. "Mr. Fairchild may like his money, but he would never stoop to obvious deception."

"Ha!" said Delores.

Mr. Magruder turned to his daughter. "My girl, have you anything to say?"

"Ha!" said Delores again.

"If that's all, then remember that silence is golden,

and that a woman's lips are more beautiful when they are resting," her father said.

Bernie agreed with his father that Delores's lips were most beautiful when she wasn't talking, but he wasn't sure about Mr. Fairchild. Maybe he *had* started the rumor. Maybe he *had* tried to drum up business for the hotel. What if the whole thing was one big fake?

Then he remembered the tapping he had heard in the night, and he wasn't so sure.

Twenty-one

Missing Delores

The following morning, Mr. and Mrs. Magruder went up to the third floor to see how the painters were doing, and Bernie tagged along.

The doors of 309 and 311 were closed, so Theodore knocked politely and waited. Soon the door opened and one of the painters peeked out. "Yes?" he said.

"I am here to inspect the rooms you have been redecorating," Mr. Magruder told him.

"And you are . . .?"

Theodore drew himself up to his full height of six feet one inch. "My good man, *I* am the manager of this hotel."

"Of course! Of course!" cried the painter, throwing the door wide open. "Do come in, sir."

Mr. and Mrs. Magruder and Bernie went into room

309 and were amazed at the change. Though the floor was still strewn with electric cord and glue and nails, three of the walls had been replastered, with crown molding around the top, new baseboard around the bottom, and they were finished with green and gold paper of peacocks in the grass. The fourth wall was in the process of being repapered with sheets of gold foil, and it looked like a room prepared for a king.

"It's beautiful!" said Mrs. Magruder. "This will be a splendid room indeed."

The painter pointed to the door in the wall leading to room 311. "The presidential suite, Ma'am. That's what Mr. Fairchild calls it."

"Absolutely splendid!" agreed Theodore. "If the president of the United States ever comes to Middleburg, I shall put him in this very room, and his wife in the room next to him. Well done, my good sirs. Can you tell me when you'll be finished?"

"Another couple days and we'll be ready for guests," said the painter.

After the Magruders had gone downstairs, Bernie said, "Why do you suppose the bankers haven't come yet, Dad?"

"We are not even to speak of them, my boy," said his father.

"But why?" Bernie asked.

"Ours is not to reason why; ours is but to do or die," said his father, which, as usual, didn't explain a thing.

Bernie had been so busy thinking about the new message that had been found on the statue in front of city hall, and the tapping he had heard during the night, that nine o'clock in the morning had come and gone and he had forgotten to keep an eye on Delores.

As soon as he got downstairs and into the apartment, Bernie went right to Delores's room. Delores wasn't there. He looked in her closet. Her clothes were gone!

Bernie rushed back out to the registration desk, where Mother was working on *The Passionate Pocketbook*.

"Mom," he whispered, "Delores is missing."

"What do you mean, 'missing'?" asked his mother. "She could be out in the yard sunning her legs. She could be in the bathroom tweezing her eyebrows. She could be in the kitchen painting her nails. She could be out on the back steps doing her exercises."

"Her clothes are gone," said Bernie.

"What?" cried Mother.

"Her closet is empty," Bernie told her.

Mother jumped up so fast that she tipped over her chair.

"Delores is gone!" Mother cried, running through the door into the family apartment. Lester and Joseph, who were having a late breakfast, jumped up and followed her down the hall to Delores's room.

"Delores is gone!" Mother cried over her shoulder to Father, as he came down the hall after them.

They crowded into Delores's room and flung open the closet door. Just as Bernie had said, the closet was empty.

"I get her room!" yelped Lester.

Theodore rapped him on the head. "Be quiet, my boy, and let me think. Who saw Delores last?"

No one, in fact, could remember seeing her that morning at all. Bernie had a sinking feeling in his stomach. Maybe the tapping he had heard in the night was not coming from the third floor at all, but was some sort of code between Delores and Raymond Tupper, about just when they would run away. As much as he wanted his sister to marry and have a happy life far away from him, Bernie knew he should have told his parents about the tapping, just in case.

"Let us not jump to hasty conclusions," Theodore was saying. "Let us not jump the gun and get left behind at the starting gate. We will all calmly, casually, go out into the lobby and inquire whether any of our guests might have seen our daughter this morning."

Bernie swallowed. They silently followed their father through the door of the apartment and out into the lobby. Old Mr. Lamkin was watching his morning show, *Name That Vegetable*. Felicity Jones was writing a poem over by the window. Mrs. Buzzwell was playing a game of solitaire at the card table, but as soon as she saw the Magruder family, she called out, "Well, Mr. Magruder, what does your daughter have to say for herself?"

"I beg your pardon?" said Theodore.

"Creeping about at all hours of the morning! I saw her, don't think I didn't."

"What was she doing?" asked Lester. "Crawling around on her hands and knees?"

"She had her suitcase with her," said Mrs. Buzzwell. "I heard the front door close about four this morning, so naturally I got out of bed and looked out, and there she was, heading right for the bus depot with the man in the red shirt."

Mother gave a little cry and swooned. She would have fallen on the floor if Theodore had not been there to catch her.

As soon as they got Mother back into the family apartment, Father said, "She must have been running away with the—"

"—great-great-great-great-great-great-grandson of Peg Leg Tupper," finished Bernie and Lester and Joseph.

Joseph immediately got the key to Raymond Tupper's room, and Bernie followed him down the hall. Joseph knocked, but no one answered. So he put the key in the lock and opened the door. The room was empty. The great-great-great-great-great-great-grandson of Peg Leg the pirate had left without paying his bill.

Twenty-two

The Presidential Suite

Now that Delores was gone, Bernie missed her. There'd be no slippers in the hall to trip over when he went to the bathroom to brush his teeth. No kimono draped over his chair when he went to the kitchen to make his toast. A family of boys without a sister.

"No telling where she is right now!" Mrs. Magruder wept. "Her married to a pirate."

"Probably walking the plank," said Lester, whereupon his father rapped him on the head once again.

"Joseph," said Father. "You and Bernie go to the bus station immediately, and see if anyone there sold a ticket to Delores last night."

The pets knew something was amiss because Lewis and Clark sat on the couch in the lobby and meowed

114

piteously. Salt Water walked nervously back and forth on his perch, squawking, "Naughty girl! Naughty girl! Awwk! Awwk!" And Mixed Blessing forlornly followed Joseph and Bernie outside.

Once on the steps, however, Bernie couldn't stand it any longer.

"Joseph." He gulped. "I think I heard Delores and Raymond Tupper signaling to each other the night before last." And he told him about the tapping.

"Listen, Bernie, if they hadn't signaled one way, they would have signaled another. It's not your fault," Joseph told him, which helped some, but not a lot.

At the ticket window, the ticket seller greeted Joseph and Bernie with a smile. "You fellas taking a trip?" he asked cheerfully.

"No," said Joseph. "I want to know if my sister came by early this morning to buy a ticket."

"Well, now, that I can't say, because I just came on duty," the man said. "Bill Gresham was on duty then, and he's in the back room having a cup of coffee before he leaves. You can go ask him, if you like."

Bernie and Joseph went to the little office behind the ticket window, where a young man was putting on his jacket.

"Could you tell me if you sold a ticket to a twenty-year-old woman with blond hair about four o'clock this morning?" Joseph asked. "She's my sister, and she seems to have disappeared."

115

"Well, now, come to think about it, I did," said the man, thoughtfully. "Yes, indeed I did."

"You did?" Bernie exclaimed hopefully. "Do you remember where she was going?"

"New Orleans," said Bill Gresham. "That was it. Yes, I'm sure of it. Her boyfriend said—"

"Boyfriend?" asked Bernie.

"Well, the man who was with her. The man in the red shirt with a gold chain around his neck. He bought a ticket for your sister to New Orleans, and I heard him say that as soon as he got down there to join her in a day or two, they would get on his boat, the *Paradise*."

"When is the next bus to New Orleans?" asked Joseph.

"Not till five o'clock tomorrow morning," Bill Gresham said. "Only one bus a day to Louisiana."

When Joseph and Bernie told their father what they had found out, Mr. Magruder said, "Well, there is only one thing to do. I must leave tomorrow morning on that bus for New Orleans and bring the girl back. Until then, I will try to get this hotel in tip-top shape so that all will run smoothly in my absence."

When Georgene and Weasel came over that afternoon, Bernie didn't feel like doing anything with them. Delores married and living in another state was one thing, but Delores sailing off on a boat named the *Paradise* with a pirate was something else.

"Maybe she'll become a pirate too," said Georgene.

"Maybe they'll capture ships together and plunder villages."

"Let's don't talk about it," said Bernie.

It was a long afternoon in the hotel that day, in spite of all the commotion out in the streets as people lined up along the walk to take their turn digging for treasure up on the hill. Mr. Magruder checked the closets to be sure there were enough clean towels and sheets while he was gone. He went over the laundry list with Hildegarde, and the faucets that needed fixing with Mr. Wilkins, and the dinner menu with Mrs. Verona.

But Mother was no help at all. Mrs. Magruder had hardly stopped crying once. She sniffled as she signed people in at the registration desk; she sobbed when she signed them out. Joseph had to give tranquilizers to the cats, who were still yowling out in the lobby, and Lester got rapped on the head for the second time in one day when his father discovered him moving his bottle-cap collection into his sister's room.

Darkness fell. Georgene and Weasel went home, and the Magruders sat solemnly around the table in the hotel apartment, eating chicken and noodles.

"D-Delores always loved chicken and noodles," wept Mother. "And to think that she may n-never eat chicken and noodles again. Not *my* chicken and noodles, anyway."

"Don't cry," said Lester. "I'll eat her share."

"If she's on a boat named *Paradise*, she's probably eating roast pheasant," said Joseph.

"We must be brave," Theodore told the family. "Just because our little bird has left the nest doesn't mean we have to fly apart; just because our little lamb has lost its fleece doesn't mean the sheep is shorn; just because one little twig is broken doesn't mean the whole tree will come crashing down. I shall put some sense into your sister's head when I find her, and I am sure she will soon be back in the bosom of the family."

About ten o'clock, everyone went to bed except Mr. Magruder. He locked the doors, wound the clock, covered the parrot's cage, and bade the guests good night. And then he sat down at the registration desk in the lobby with his suitcase beside him to wait until it was time to go to the bus depot and buy his ticket to New Orleans.

Bernie was just about to doze off when he heard a noise and his eyes popped open. He listened.

Tap . . . tap, tap . . . tap, tap, tap, . . . tap . . .

He sat up. He could hear Lester snoozing away in the bunk below. He crept quietly out of bed and tiptoed to the registration desk, where his father was sitting.

"Dad," he whispered. "I hear a noise."

"What kind of a noise?" asked Theodore, not even looking up from his newspaper.

"A tapping. Like . . . like someone tapping on a wall, maybe. I heard it the night before last too."

Mr. Magruder put down his newspaper and listened. "By Jove, I believe I do hear something," he said. "It seems to be coming from the third floor."

"That's what I thought," said Bernie.

Together, Bernie and his father went up the stairs to second. They turned at the landing and went up the stairs to third. The tapping seemed to be coming from room 309.

"That is very strange indeed," whispered Father to Bernie. "The painters have gone home for the day. Wait here, Bernie, while I get the key."

It was the longest two minutes Bernie had ever waited, but at last his father was back with the key and a flashlight. Softly Mr. Magruder turned the key in the lock, and opened the door to the room. Bernie clicked on the flashlight.

There stood Raymond Tupper, the great-great-great-great-great-great-grandson of Peg Leg Tupper, with a hammer in one hand, his other hand deep down inside the wall.

Twenty-three

A Daughter Returns

"You scoundrel!" cried Theodore. "What have you done with my daughter?"

Raymond Tupper's mouth dropped open.

"Mr. Magruder, sir, I can explain," he said. "I am about to make your daughter a very rich woman indeed!" And he pulled his hand out of the wall, opened his fingers, and there, in his palm, sat five pieces of gold.

Bernie stared.

"Gold!" said Raymond Tupper. "This is where my great-great-great-great-great-great-grandfather Peg Leg buried his gold—right here in the wall of 309." With his hammer, he gently tapped at the wall again, knocking out still another piece of plaster, and this time he brought up a few more coins.

"How did you know it was here?" asked Father.

"I came into the possession of a map in which Peg Leg shows the gold to be in your hotel. I knew there were rumors for as long as I could remember that the gold was somewhere in Middleburg, but no one knew where it was. If word got out that I was coming to get it, I feared someone would find it before me. So I left notes about town, suggesting that the gold was buried on Bessledorf Hill."

Bernie was terribly disappointed. "You just made them up?"

"Stem to stern, all nonsense," said Raymond. "Every day I'd check the place I'd left a note the day before, and if it was gone, I simply left another. Drove the police crazy, I'm afraid. All but the notes in the couch, which you found, I suspect."

"Who were they for?"

"The painters, of course! I go by the nickname of Jet Lag, you see, so that's what they called me. We didn't necessarily want anyone to know we were in on this together, so when we had to talk, we left notes in the couch."

"But what did they mean?" Bernie asked.

"Well, we'd worked out a few code words that we used over and over again. 'S.W.' meant 'Slow work,' 'N.L.' meant 'No luck,' 'P,' of course, stood for 'Painters,' and 'K.T.' meant 'Keep trying.' When a number was mentioned, it was the time the painters quit for the night."

"But those first holes *we* found on Bessledorf Hill!" said Bernie.

"Oh, yes, I went over there a few times to dig some holes, and added small ones as well, just the size of a pirate's peg leg. All of that was to divert attention to Bessledorf Hill so that I could search for my great-great-great-great-great-great-grandfather's treasure here in peace. And now I have found what is rightfully mine."

"And the painters?" asked Theodore. "Where do they fit in?"

"I had to have help," said Raymond. "I wasn't the only one who had a copy of that map, and when I heard that these chaps were looking too, I told them I would pay for the wallpaper and remodeling if they would pose as painters and help find where in the walls the gold was hidden. When we found it, we would split it three ways."

"Then why are you here alone, in the middle of the night, with your hand in the wall?" asked Theodore. "And what have you done with my daughter?"

"It's all for Delores, Mr. Magruder," said Raymond Tupper, putting his hand inside the wall again. "I want her to live like a queen. I want her to . . ." But he never finished, because when he pulled his hand out of the wall a second time, he was holding a gun.

Bernie's heart almost jumped out of his chest.

"Just like your daughter, sir, you ask too many questions," Raymond Tupper said. "I had to buy her a ticket to New Orleans and promise to take her on my boat, the *Paradise*, to get her out of my way. Don't make a sound, if you want to live. Stand with your backs together, hands in the air."

Bernie and his father did as they were told, and Raymond Tupper took some electric cord that was lying about and began tying them together.

"By the time anyone comes to find you," Raymond went on, "I shall be on my way to Spain or France with half a million in gold. This town can go on digging till Doomsday for all I care."

"But what about my daughter?" muttered Theodore angrily.

This time Raymond Tupper thrust the gun against Theodore's side, and Bernie almost cried out, he was so afraid that his father might be shot.

"No questions, sir. Your daughter will find out soon enough that she's on the *Paradise* by herself, don't you worry. Now if you will be so kind as to let me remove your tie so that I can bind your hands together . . ."

"Freeze!" yelled a voice from the doorway, and when Bernie jerked his head around, he saw the two painters coming into the room with guns.

"Drop it!" the first painter yelled to Raymond Tupper, and the pirate's gun clattered to the floor.

"Having a little party without us, Ray?" asked the first painter.

"Getting a little greedy, are we?" said the second.

"You men are not painters at all, but thieving, lying robbers and cheats!" cried Theodore, angry at them all. "Is Mr. Fairchild in on this too?"

"Mr. Fairchild doesn't know a bloomin' thing," said the second painter. "We concocted the letter to you ourselves so you would let us work on these rooms. And just as we figured, you didn't suspect a thing, because why would you question two men who were coming to make an improvement in your hotel? There are no bankers arriving, and all that 'high and lively' talk was hogwash. You can put your hands down now, sir, because we're not about to shoot you." Bernie was very glad indeed to hear that, because his arms were getting tired. He and his father began untying themselves. But the two painters kept their guns on Raymond Tupper.

"The fact is," the first painter continued, "that gold doesn't belong to this fellow at all because he is no relation to Peg Leg. *We* are."

"*You?*" cried Bernie.

"Yes, *we* are the great-great-great-great-great-great-grandsons of Peg Leg Tupper, and this scoundrel you see before you is neither Raymond Tupper nor Jet Lag, but the great-great-great-great-great-great-grandson of Jean Laffite, one of the most notorious pirates to sail the seven seas, and Peg Leg's number one enemy."

"What?" cried Theodore.

Raymond Tupper glared at them darkly.

"We knew all along that if you ever found out where that gold was hidden, you would be after it in a flash," one of the painters said to Raymond. "We've been keeping an eye on you, don't think we haven't. When we heard the rumor that you had found a copy of the map drawn by our great-great-great-great-great-great-grandfather, we struck up a conversation with you, gained your confidence, and, just as we hoped, you let us in on the secret. But you weren't about to share the gold with anyone, were you? Not to mention the fact that it doesn't belong to you in the first place."

"I shall not have scoundrels in my hotel!" said Theodore, shaking his fist in Raymond Tupper's face. "And you, sir, left without paying your bill."

"I'll pay you in gold," said Raymond Tupper, his hands still over his head.

"Not with *our* gold, you won't," said one of the painters. "This gold belongs to the descendants of our great-great-great-great-great-great-grandfather, not the descendants of Jean Laffite."

"Wrong!" came another voice from the doorway, and there stood Officer Feeney, with gun number four. "Drop your weapons, please." Two more guns fell to the floor.

"Saw the light on up here and came to see what was the matter. Heard the whole danged conversation, and if you three aren't a sorry sight. The gold doesn't belong to any one of you, because it never belonged to Peg Leg, either. He *stole* the gold, my lads, and so it belongs to the United States government. I believe we have three empty beds at the county jail, and we'll see what the judge has to say in the morning."

Just then there were footsteps in the hallway, and suddenly there stood Delores.

"Delores, my darling daughter!" cried Theodore.

"You've come back!" said Raymond Tupper, beginning to perspire.

"Indeed I have, you low-down, double-crossing excuse for a pirate!" Delores said, marching across the room and hitting him over the head with her pocketbook. "You thought you could send me to New Orleans to get rid of me, didn't you? You thought you could sweet-talk me into anything. Well, on the bus, I just happened to sit down beside an old sea captain who had been visiting his sister here in Middleburg. When I asked if he knew of a boat named *Paradise*, he threw back his head and said indeed he did—it was the oldest, dirtiest boat in the harbor, its deck rotten to the core, and leaking so badly that they simply sank it—that it was down at the bottom of the sea.

"I told the driver to let me off the bus, and caught the first one coming back. You are a scumbag, whoever you are, and I shall be happy if I never see another great-great-great-great-great-great-grandson of a pirate as long as I live."

"Wow!" said Bernie. Even he couldn't have said it better.

When the newspaper carried the story the next day, it said that the great-great-great-great-great-great-grandson of Jean Laffite, also known as Raymond Tupper, would be going back to New Orleans to work on a shrimp boat after his six months in jail, that the real great-great-great-great-great-great-grandsons of Peg Leg Tupper were taking up real estate after they had faced their own charges, and that Delores Magruder, after a brief absence, had returned to the bosom of her family.

Actually, the painters/treasure seekers were ordered to finish the redecorating they had begun at the Bessledorf Hotel before they could go. So Mr. Fairchild, to his delight, had two rooms beautifully redone at no cost to himself. The city put Bessledorf Hill back together again; the cats quit meowing; Mrs. Magruder stopped crying and began working once more on her book; Delores got her room back after Lester moved his bottle-cap collection out; the town of Middleburg sent the gold to the U.S. Treasury; and Bernie, Georgene, and Weasel still sat on the wall at the back of the garden when they hadn't anything better to do.

And sometimes, when the neighborhood was quiet, they thought that they could hear the sound of tapping—the sound of a man with a peg leg—walking slowly, carefully, along the alley.

Mysterious things are always going on at the Bessledorf Hotel. Don't miss any of **Phyllis Reynolds Naylor's** other zany adventures featuring Bernie Magruder and his friends: